MW00943716

Sweet Afternoons

Blueberry Beach Novels, Volume 6

Jessie Gussman

Published by Jessie Gussman, 2021.

Cover art by Julia Gussman
Editing by Heather Hayden[1]
Narration by Jay Dyess[2]

~~~

Click HERE[3] if you'd like to subscribe to my newsletter and find out why people say "Jessie's is the only newsletter I open and read."

~~~

1.   https://hhaydeneditor.com/

2.   https://www.facebook.com/SayWithJay

3. https://BookHip.com/FASFD

Chapter 1

Drake Jensen stood on the ladder in the foyer of the Indigo Inn in Blueberry Beach, Michigan, stretching out as far as he could and dabbing white paint on the water spot on the ceiling.

Some kind of major catastrophe had happened upstairs in the bedroom just above where he now worked, with water leaking into the floor and staining the ceiling.

The bedroom had been fixed, but there was going to be a wedding next week at the inn, and he was trying to make things look as good as he could.

Leiklyn and Ethan deserved to have the inn look its very best. They also deserved every bit of happiness they could get.

Although Drake had been to much bigger, much fancier weddings—the folks in Hollywood knew how to throw a big bash—he hadn't seen too many couples who had the deep respect, firm commitment, and absolute love that Leiklyn and Ethan displayed.

He wanted to do everything in his power to make their special day perfect.

And that meant moving the ladder one more time.

There was a small spot just out of reach that needed some paint yet.

He climbed down the ladder, looking around at the foyer with pride.

He'd just finished installing the new stone tiles on the floor himself.

Before he'd made it big in Hollywood, doing stone tile floors had been one of his dad's specialties in his construction business.

Drake had put more than one floor in, but there weren't any that he was more proud of.

It was a light blue color with swirled gray highlights.

The color of Lake Michigan on a hot summer day.

The color of the Michigan sky in September.

The color of ripe blueberries just touched by the morning dew.

gether. "I just finished putting the flooring in earlier this week. I have to admit it's kinda hard to see it looking like that."

"I'm so sorry. Normally, I'm not quite that clumsy." The woman's tones were subdued but still cultured. "While you get the rags, maybe I can search the internet for how to get paint off of tile. That's what this is?"

"That's right. Stone tile." He took two steps before the dog prints stopped him. "What happened to your dog?"

"Myla, Leiklyn's daughter, was sitting on the back porch. I asked her to keep an eye on Ruffles until I get the mess cleaned up. She's going to clean off her paws too."

"So...the dog's a girl?" Drake asked, not sure why it mattered. Other than the dog had looked regal. He supposed he should have known it was a girl.

"Yeah." She lifted a shoulder. "She was a stray that showed up at a funeral I attended."

He laughed despite himself.

She continued. "She followed me home, and I've never had a dog before, but she kind of adopted me. A craft store across the street from where my apartment was had the name Rags and Ruffles." She smiled affectionately. "While she looked more like the rag part of that, I named her Ruffles."

"She seems like a pretty nice dog. She's loyal anyway," he said, remembering how the dog looked at him like imploring him to apologize before following her mistress out into the hall. He didn't really believe that dogs were almost human, the way so many people, particularly in Hollywood, did, but Ruffles was almost enough to make him change his mind.

He walked out, gathering the rags and a bucket of water, and headed back to the foyer.

It took them half an hour, but by the time they were finished, the foyer looked almost as good as new.

There was a little bit of paint that had dried on the cement between the stone tiles that they were unable to get off, but otherwise, he couldn't tell that paint had been spilled.

Willan threw her last rag in the bucket as Drake stood and offered her his hand.

"It doesn't look too bad. I thought for sure the floor was ruined," she said, allowing him to help her, then standing with her hands on her hips, her eyes scanning the floor.

"I appreciate you helping." It was on the tip of his tongue to say he admired her for being willing to get down on her hands and knees and work, but although they'd kept up a rather steady chatter about the weather and the tourist season in Blueberry Beach, he didn't figure he knew her that well. Plus, if she figured out who he was, he didn't want her to think that he'd been hitting on her or anything of that nature.

He'd been warned more than once that a man with his amount of wealth needed to be very careful about what he said and what he did, as there were a lot of gold diggers who would make unfounded accusations, or take anything he might say out of context, or even make up lies about him.

Willan didn't seem like that kind of person, but he did know from the gossip that he'd overheard here and there that the inn was in some financial trouble. Sometimes when people needed money, they would stoop to doing things that they normally wouldn't.

Part of him was sure that Willan would never do such a thing, was aghast that he would even consider it of her, and part of him, the practical part, said that a man in his position could never be too careful.

"Well, I guess I better go get my dog," Willan said, after a somewhat uncomfortable silence where he reminded himself that he couldn't get too close to people. Especially people he didn't know.

"Yeah. Thanks again for coming back out," he said, knowing everything he had just told himself to be true yet wondering why it was so hard for him to dismiss the lady and walk away.

Maybe because she seemed genuinely friendly and nice.

Or maybe, he admired someone who could apologize.

In his experience, women, or maybe people in general, usually thought they were right and weren't afraid to let everyone around them know it.

Shaking his head, he lifted a hand, then walked out the front door with the bucket, intending to bring the rags out and come back in and get his ladder and put everything away.

The foyer looked fantastic again. Thankfully. But there was still plenty of work to do before the wedding.

Chapter 2

"Thanks so much for watching Ruffles," Willan said to Myla as she stepped out on the back porch, closing the door softly behind her.

The man in the foyer had seemed familiar. Not just his looks, which honestly she really thought she'd seen him somewhere before, but his personality.

She just felt...not comfortable, exactly, with him but almost like being with him felt right in some way.

It was an odd feeling and one she tried to dismiss as her overactive imagination.

Coming to Blueberry Beach, getting to be a part of Ethan and Leiklyn's wedding, was such an honor, and she was so excited about it, but she wanted to find her own forever love.

The reality of the wedding and her thoughts about finding her own life partner had made her more inclined to look at the man and see what she wanted to see or, in her case, feel what she wanted to feel.

She hadn't ever been interested in rough-looking, bearded men.

There was her perfectionist side coming out again. Like the man she wanted had to look exactly the way she'd imagined him in her daydreams. If he didn't, she wasn't interested.

She was truly trying to get over that.

"She's a sweet girl," Myla said. "She seems to be pretty protective of my kittens." Myla nodded her head at the dog and the box beside her.

Sure enough, Ruffles crouched beside the kittens, her nose over the box, her ears perked up, and her whole body saying she would throw herself in front of a runaway freight train in order to save them.

Willan had made sure that Ruffles had been fixed before she kept her.

It made her smile to see that Ruffles didn't need puppies of her own in order for her mothering instincts to come out.

She didn't even need puppies.

Kittens would do.

Myla put a hand over her stomach and stretched her back. She seemed tired, and Willan figured it was time for her to find her friend.

"Do you know where your mom is?" she asked, straightening back up.

"She's in the dining room getting ready for the ladies' luncheon."

"Oh. I don't want to interrupt anything. I guess I'll..." She wasn't sure what she was going to do. She had been planning on staying at the inn. Leiklyn had said that they might have an extra room, although the rooms were filling up as fast as they could get them finished.

Willan hadn't made any other plans though. Maybe because she found it unbelievable that the inn would be so popular.

"I'm sure you can go on in and join them. It's not really a formal thing, although 'luncheon' makes it sound that way. It's just Mom and Miss Iva May, and sometimes there is another lady or two who comes to eat and talk. Nothing special," Myla said, lifting her shoulder. "I like to go because the food is good, but I think today I'll skip it. I need to feed and water our chickens, and I'm going to take a nap."

The girl stood up, her baby bump prominent under her T-shirt as she stepped away from the box of kittens.

"The dining room's just through the kitchen. If you don't mind, can you find it yourself?"

"I'm sure I can. You go ahead and get your work done and take it easy," Willan said, amazed at how much Myla looked like her mother as a teenager.

She supposed she'd never really had any desire to have a child just to have someone who looked like her, but as she'd gotten older, the desire just to have a baby to hold in her arms had been more and more prominent. A child to look at her and call her "mom."

Unfortunately, it was her own fault that her life hadn't gone that way.

Checking Ruffles's paws, she saw that they were clean and dry. Ruffles didn't want to leave the box of kittens, and Willan had a good mind to just leave her there.

"I think Ruffles would be pretty happy to sit beside the box of kittens for the rest of the day," she said, and Myla laughed.

"I agree. If you like, leave her there. I'll keep an eye on her and let you know if she wanders off the porch."

It didn't look like Ruffles was going to wander anywhere, so Willan nodded her thanks and went back in the house.

The dining room wasn't hard to find, and she stepped in. Her mouth dropped. The ceiling was high, giving the room a huge, airy look. Even the massive solid wood table couldn't make it seem dark or dreary.

Big bay windows opened up, showing a gorgeous view of the blue serenity of Lake Michigan.

"Willan!" Leiklyn exclaimed from the sidebar where she was arranging what looked like bologna sandwiches.

Willan smiled, glad that Leiklyn hadn't evolved into someone fancy and untouchable, even though the inn kind of gave off that vibe.

"It is so gorgeous in here," Willan said as she walked forward, wrapping her arms around Leiklyn and squeezing. "And you are just absolutely beaming."

"Thank you. Thank you so much. I feel like I'm glowing from the inside out. There is a part of me that regrets that this didn't happen a long time ago, and it's all my stupidity. But even more of me is just so excited that it's happening now," Leiklyn said as she pulled back.

Truly, her eyes glowed, her cheeks were rosy, and happiness seemed to radiate off of her.

"I don't know if I've ever seen anyone as beautiful as you." Willan didn't really mean classic beauty but all the bright light of happiness that seemed to shine straight from Leiklyn. Happiness that made the whole room feel warm and inviting and beautiful.

"No one has ever accused me of being beautiful," Leiklyn said.

"You're beautiful." A deep voice came from the doorway, causing them both to turn.

Leiklyn dropped her arms from around Willan and didn't quite run to the man Willan recognized as Ethan, her fiancé.

Willan was pretty sure they'd probably seen each other at least once that day, but their embrace kind of made it seem like it had been years instead of minutes or possibly hours since they'd last laid eyes on each other.

"I won't keep you. Just wanted to look at you for a minute." Ethan grinned, and then he nodded at Willan and greeted her.

Willan replied and then waited as Ethan said a few words to Leiklyn before he walked out. "He seems pretty happy too. Although I don't think his glow quite matches yours."

"That's because I'm getting the better end of the bargain," Leiklyn said, with no trace of bitterness or envy.

"I think it's just because his tan hides it a little more than yours does," Willan speculated.

"You could be right." Leiklyn laughed. "Miss Iva May is coming, and maybe a few other ladies, to eat and chat. I hope you can stay, and maybe until they get here, you and I can catch up some?"

Willan nodded, and they pulled out chairs at the big table, sitting and talking about the weather and Willan's trip for a couple of minutes.

"The inn seems rather busy," Willan said, just as they heard another door shut and footsteps in the hall.

"It has been! I've been surprised. I didn't realize demand would be so high. We should have done this years ago," Leiklyn gushed.

Willan couldn't disagree. She should have taken charge of her life years ago, too.

"I'll admit it's gotten crazy. I didn't realize how much time I would spend helping guests. They become like family while they're here. I love it!"

Chapter 3

Before Willan could answer Leiklyn, the dining room door opened, and a lady with short dark hair stepped in, followed by a tall blond man and two preteen kids.

"Leiklyn?" the lady said in a calm tone that belied the frazzled look on her face.

Leiklyn stood from her chair. "Yes, Selena? Is there something I can do for you?"

"We wanted to go swim in the lake, but we left our towels at home. Do you have towels for sale here?"

"We don't have any here at the inn, but many of the shops in Blueberry Beach carry them. The surf shop in particular has a really good selection," Leiklyn said.

"I can pick some up, if you want to take the kids on down," the man suggested from his position slightly behind Selena.

"Don't be silly," Selena snapped, although Willan wasn't sure she meant to sound quite as sharp as what she did. "We don't want to go down to the beach without towels. You'd probably end up stopping to talk to someone, anyway, and we'll be there this afternoon, and still no towels." She rolled her eyes and chuckled a bit, looking at Leiklyn and Willan like she expected them to laugh along with her.

Willan didn't want to be rude, but she felt bad for Selena's husband. While it's possible that the man really would find someone to talk to and never show up with towels, Selena's words weren't said very nicely.

The man's lips pressed together, and maybe there was some irritation on his face, but his whole demeanor said he just wanted to help the family have a good vacation. "Then I guess we can all go together."

"I don't feel like walking the whole way to Blueberry Beach. You go get the towels, and I'll stay here with the children. They can watch another cartoon until you get back." She began to turn, then stopped short. "Don't take too long."

The man nodded at his wife and turned to walk out. "I'll be right back."

"Daddy, can I go with you?" the little boy asked.

"No, Earl. You're dressed for the beach, not for shopping. You come back upstairs with me." Selena grabbed the little boy's hand, then took the girl's hand as well.

"But I want to go with Daddy. I never get to."

"We'll go with Daddy to the beach," Selena said shortly. She looked over her shoulder. "Thanks, Leiklyn. This inn is just fabulous. My friends are so jealous over all of my great beach pics. I'm glad we found it."

"We're happy to have you here. Let me know if you need anything," Leiklyn said, slipping back down into her chair.

The door closed behind them, and they sat in silence for a bit.

It was on the tip of Willan's tongue to say to Leiklyn if she ever got married, she didn't want Leiklyn to allow her to treat her husband like that. But she didn't. That would be unkind and almost gossipy.

But she really didn't think Selena realized how snippy she was coming off and could maybe benefit from a friend's wise counsel.

"I think..." Leiklyn began, fingering the pile of napkins that were sitting on the table. "I think sometimes we have a tendency to take advantage of people around us. The people we're familiar with and at ease with. We lose some of our manners, maybe, around them, and instead of treating the people that we love and who are close to us better than everyone else, we treat them worse."

That's exactly what Willan had been thinking. Just stated in a much nicer way.

"We put a little veneer on ourselves for the rest of the world to see, but it comes off when we're home around the people we truly care about." Not that she really had much experience in that, since she lived by herself, but she agreed with Leiklyn. Thinking back on her family life, maybe her mother hadn't hated her like she'd always thought but had just been so comfortable at home she forgot to be nice?

"Yes. In some respects, we want to be able to be ourselves and be comfortable in our own homes. But I think people can start to wonder if we really like them, since we put so much effort into impressing others and no effort into impressing them." She laughed a little. "Please excuse me. I've been thinking about marriage and some of the reasons that people don't stay married."

"A lack of commitment," Willan said immediately.

"Of course. That's a huge one, but other people just drift apart. And I don't want that to happen to me. But it's easy for me to sit here and say that I'm always going to treat Ethan better than any other person, but...will I really?"

"It's probably a decision that we have to get up and make every morning," Willan said, slowly, because she was thinking about it. She didn't have any experience in being married or staying married, although she'd certainly seen her share of couples who had gotten married and gotten divorced over the years.

There were lessons to be learned in marriages that failed, just as much as there were lessons to be learned in marriages that succeeded.

"I think the very fact you're thinking about it means you care, and that's part of staying together."

"I hope." She looked past Willan's shoulder, her mind seeming to be far away. "Right now, I want to be the best wife I can for Ethan. But...I wonder if that will wear off? If I'm going to stop worrying about being a good wife and worry more about life? About the impression I make on strangers? Making them happy rather than making my family my focus. Even my children. I can see where I've done that at times. Being more concerned about what my children's friends' parents think of me than actually thinking about what's best for my children and how I'm treating them." She shook her head. "I don't even think I'm making any sense."

"You know I don't have children. So I can't really say, but I know at the library, some patrons come in every week and I know it doesn't matter how I treat them, they're coming back. Not that I was ever mean to anyone, but I know I don't have to go out of my way to make conversation and make them laugh or feel comfortable. But some people, especially if it's their first time, I feel like I need to give them extra special attention, and that might mean some of the regulars get neglected."

"Exactly. I've caught myself doing that with the inn guests. It's like my family are the regulars."

"Back when I was a young mother," a new voice said from the doorway.

Willan's head jerked around. She hadn't seen Iva May standing there.

She started to rise, but Iva May put her hand up. "When I was a young mother," she began again, "I had a friend who told me that her children watched her answer the door and talk to a delivery person as he made his delivery. When she shut the door and turned around, her children were staring at her, and one of them said, "Mom? Why aren't you as nice to Daddy as you are to that man? Do you love him better than Daddy?" Iva May shook her head. "That story has stuck with me through the years. I don't want to be nicer to anyone than I am to the people living in my home. To the people who are close to me. To the people I work with every day. What's the point in giving a good impression to strangers if the impression I give to my family and coworkers is that they're less than a stranger and unimportant?"

"Wise words as always, Miss Iva May," Leiklyn said, standing and walking to the older lady and giving her a hug.

Willan followed, and they chatted for a bit before Iva May came in and sat down.

"That was a pretty deep subject for such a beautiful morning." Iva May folded her hands on the table and seemed to be referring to what they had been talking about when she walked in.

"It seems like a good subject for someone who's getting married next week," Leiklyn said, walking over to the sidebar where she'd placed the food.

"And sometimes we see things and we think to ourselves 'I don't want that to be me,'" Willan said, not wanting to talk about Selena but knowing that that's what sparked the idea in her own mind.

After all, she was far from having any kind of thoughts of marriage in her future.

"I think it's impossible to be too nice to your spouse or your family. Or your friends for that matter. Good reminder." Her smile said she was pleased that the two of them were taking the way they treated people seriously. Then, she looked around the room. "So what's going on with the inn? It looks like the foyer has been painted, are there more rooms available?" Iva May asked as Leiklyn brought the platter of sandwiches to the table.

"The rooms are filling up as fast as we can get them ready."

"That's great." Iva May took a sandwich triangle from the platter. "I know the diner has been so much busier since the inn opened up."

"I'm glad. It makes me happy that opening the inn has benefited the shops in Blueberry Beach. I certainly would have been terribly upset if we had taken business away instead of adding to it."

"I don't see how it could have been anything but beneficial." Iva May's gaze turned to Willan. "Is there a room for you?"

Willan turned to Leiklyn, who bit her lip, and her face looked a little scrunched up.

"We hadn't gotten to that point yet. I guess we've been too busy talking about abstract ideas and hadn't gotten to anything concrete."

Willan considered that she might have to find somewhere else to stay. "I'm so happy the inn is so busy!" She laughed. "I hadn't thought I might need to find somewhere else to stay, but I can't be upset that the inn is so popular."

"We do have a room that's supposed to be finished today. I also have a waiting list of people to call who want the next available room."

"But you haven't called them yet, right?" Iva May said.

"No. Willan gets the first spot, of course."

"I'm sorry. The people who are subleasing my apartment wanted to move in earlier than I had anticipated. So it's my fault, because I told you I probably wouldn't be here until a couple of days before the wedding, and I showed up a week early."

"That's okay. Just because we have a waiting list doesn't mean we have to call them," Leiklyn said sincerely.

"But I know we could use the money. Although..." Willan smiled at Leiklyn and then Iva May. "I came into an unexpected inheritance..." Her face fell for just a minute. "I also brought a dog, which really has nothing to do with anything, but I probably should admit that right off."

Leiklyn's face scrunched up again. "We're not allowed to have dogs, other than service animals, in the inn, since we serve food here. State regulations."

"I thought there might be a problem like that. She's out on the porch right now, although she did walk through the spilled paint in the foyer."

"Someone spilled paint in the foyer?" Leiklyn said, putting her hands on the table and pushing back.

Willam put her hand up in the universal sign for "stop." "Don't worry about it. It's all taken care of. But Ruffles, my dog, did walk through it. We got that cleaned up too. And she's outside guarding the kittens. She seems to want to adopt them, I think."

"That's sweet," Leiklyn said, a little disbelief in her voice but coupled with a note that said that a dog wanting to adopt kittens was cute.

"What about the inheritance that you mentioned?" Iva May said, getting the conversation back to the important thing.

"My aunt Tabitha, whom I really didn't know very well, passed away, and I was rather shocked to find that she willed everything she owned, which was worth a rather substantial sum of money, to me."

"That's like something everyone dreams about. Coming into an unexpected inheritance!" Leiklyn's eyes glowed. "I'm so happy for you!"

Willan nodded, thinking that maybe she would have rather found her soulmate than gotten an inheritance. But still, she could do some good with the inheritance here in Blueberry Beach and for her friends. Maybe the soulmate thing just wasn't going to happen for her.

"I guess my dreams came true," she said, a tiny bit of sarcasm in her voice.

Iva May's kindly blue eyes narrowed just a bit, like she had picked up on Willan's sarcasm and saw through her smile to the woman who wanted to find a man who would love her for what she was underneath. The woman who longed for that. The woman who knew that it was her own fault she hadn't found it, since she hadn't thought herself perfect enough to deserve such a man. Not to mention, she'd been picky about the kind of man she wanted.

Not a mountain man.

The guy with the overgrown beard out in the foyer, the painter, flashed through her mind.

She wasn't going to be picky. Although, that's the kind of man she never would have been happy with before.

Before she decided that she was going to stop having certain expectations of what she should have and be open to the idea that just as she wasn't perfect, the man she married wouldn't be perfect either.

And maybe she had been looking for perfection when what she really needed was imperfection.

"I don't want you to feel that you came into an inheritance and you have to use it to fix up the inn." Leiklyn grunted. "You could use it for anything. Go anywhere. I don't know how much you got, but you could totally use it for yourself."

"You're not interrupting. We've got some bologna sandwiches if you'd like one."

There were at least three sandwiches sitting on the tray, and it looked like all of the ladies had eaten, if the crumbs in front of them were any indication.

So he said, "Thanks," and walked forward, snagging a sandwich. "Do you have a minute to talk to me, Leiklyn?"

"I do, of course. Do you need me to go somewhere else?"

"No," he said, a little uncertainly.

For some reason, his eyes tracked to Willan, who was sitting across the table from Miss Iva May. The woman had made him angry, angrier than he could recall being in a long time, but he'd actually enjoyed cleaning up the paint with her.

Anyone who could make cleaning up spilled paint fun was someone he wouldn't mind spending time with.

Willan was just that kind of woman.

Plus, he appreciated the fact that she didn't look like she starved herself and that she seemed like a nice, down-to-earth kind person.

Regardless, he pulled his eyes away and focused on Leiklyn. "No. Not at all. And it won't take very long. I just got a call from my ex-wife. She's already loaded the kids up on a plane along with a flight nanny, and they're going to be arriving at O'Hare in just a few hours. I need to leave right now so I'll be there when they arrive."

"Of course! Is there anything you need me to do?" Leiklyn asked, her brows knitted.

"No. But unfortunately, I probably won't be able to continue to help with the renovations, at least for a while, because my kids aren't old enough to be on their own without supervision."

"How old are they?" Leiklyn asked.

If she was upset that the renovations were going to be stalled, she didn't show it. Instead, her concern seemed to be for him and his children.

"Five and seven," he said. "I do apologize. I know that you and Ethan were really counting on me to help you get the inn ready. I know you have a waiting list for rooms, and Ethan has a whole schedule that he was hoping to adhere to. I'm just not going to be able to."

"I totally understand. Your children come first, of course." Leiklyn's smile was genuine. "And you absolutely want to be there when they land. Although, this seems unexpected."

"It certainly is. I don't want to say anything unkind about my ex, but let's just say sometimes when people break up, they use their kids as tools to hurt their spouse rather than realizing the kids have feelings of their own."

"I see."

He figured she probably did. Who hadn't been around someone who'd been through a messy divorce?

Isla had taken the children with her when she left him for the nanny, and he figured it was mostly because she thought that would be the most hurtful thing.

He'd been in the process of fighting to see them through his lawyer. So her call was welcome. He wasn't going to be shut out of his kids' lives just because his ex changed her mind about wanting him, hurtful as that was.

Her phone message had been cryptic, but reading between the lines, their two young children were cramping on her budding romance, and she didn't want to be bothered.

"While I'm on my way to Chicago, I'll see what I can do about finding someone to watch the kids." Nannies weren't hard to find in LA, but he'd never been the one to do the hiring. Normally, he'd call someone to do it for him, but if he didn't want the press to catch wind of where he was and what he was doing, he needed to keep contact with his Hollywood personnel to a minimum.

He was a grown man. He could find a nanny.

"Depending on how long it takes me to hire someone, I'd like to be back to work within a week or so. I know that's going to slow down the preparations for the wedding, and I'm sorry about that, but..." He shrugged. There wasn't anything he could do.

"I can watch them."

All the eyes in the room went to Willan.

"Are you a professional nanny?" he asked, although he wasn't sure why. It wasn't like he would only consider hiring a professional nanny.

"No. I was a librarian until I resigned last week."

He jerked his head in a short nod. He would not have guessed that she was a librarian. He wasn't sure why.

"I can vouch for her, if you're interested in taking her up on that," Leiklyn said. "I've known her since she was in high school. Although we've lost touch over the years, she's a good person, and she'd be great with your kids."

"You have kids of your own?"

Funny how a person could ask personal questions like that when they were interviewing for a job. He found himself more than a little curious about the answer.

"I don't." She seemed to want to say more, and he got the feeling that not having children was a sore spot for her.

He swallowed before saying, "Husband?"

That was a little out of the bounds of what might be appropriate for him to ask, but he supposed it could be relevant. "If your husband's going to be around the children, I'd like to have references and clearances from him as well as you." There. That seemed to justify his question.

"No husband. And I had to have clearances to work at the library. I can give you those."

"That'll work. So you worked with children at the library?"

"Of course. We had a very nice children's section, and I spent a lot of time in it."

This could almost be too good to be true. It was funny that he had just been thinking how much he enjoyed working with her, and now...

"I was thinking full-time nanny. Someone who would live with m...the children." He'd almost said "me" but realized just in time that didn't sound the best.

It occurred to him having a live-in nanny was not what the rest of the world did. Certainly, with his working-class background, he was familiar with babysitters, of course, but not nannies. Nannies who basically raised the children and were on call twenty-four/seven.

"That should be fine. I would have a day off, of course?"

"Of course. We'd have to work that out." He glanced around the table. "I'm willing to be flexible if you are, and we don't have to waste any more of your time."

"That's fine." Her lips pulled back into what could be considered a smile. "Maybe you want to see if the children like me okay?"

Of course. He hadn't considered that. To cover what should have been an obvious concern, he asked, "Do you usually have a problem with children liking you?"

"I never have. But wouldn't that be something you'd want to make sure of?"

He gave an internal sigh. He was an actor, but he didn't like giving off impressions that weren't honest in his real life. Being truthful was always the best policy. "I'll just be honest, I've never been in charge of hiring a nanny before."

"So you've had nannies in the past?" Willan asked immediately.

He could have slapped his forehead. She didn't know who he was, and he didn't want them to know.

Maybe he'd given away more than he should have since he'd been concerned with finding a nanny so he could get back to work. A common laborer like he was supposed to be, a painter, builder, shouldn't be hiring nannies.

Standing with her hand on the banister, at the top of the stairs, watching his car pull in.

He hadn't promised her money, hadn't even told her what he would pay her, hadn't said anything other than he'd accepted her offer to help, and she said she'd be there.

And she was.

Maybe that was a little thing, but it was huge to him.

To have someone do something they said they were going to do, not because it benefited them, not because they're getting something out of it, just because they said they would.

He pulled the car to a stop and put the transmission in park, turning the motor off.

Maybe Willan had ulterior motives, but she'd offered to be his nanny before she knew who he was.

She started walking down the steps as he opened his door, and he looked at her once more.

He didn't want to believe that she had shown up for any other reason than she wanted to keep her word.

Or maybe that she'd liked him. The real him. That would be even better.

She wasn't model thin or movie-star gorgeous, and as far as he understood, she had absolutely no dreams or plans of becoming a star, and so she wouldn't need him, wouldn't need his help.

Those were the only things he could think of that would make her want to use him.

So he almost had to believe that she was here because she said she would be. That she was helping because she wanted to be kind. That she wasn't expecting anything in return, since she didn't even know if he was going to pay her minimum wage or not.

He closed the door carefully and waited for her to walk up to him.

"They're both asleep. I had to buy car seats, but they came with a bunch of other luggage." He indicated the door behind him.

"Kids seem to require a lot of stuff," she said softly, and her voice was just as he remembered, not wildly romantic, or husky and sexy, but just a little low and perfectly right.

"Hazel's on that side, and Kimbi's on this one. Kimbi's the seven-year-old," he said as she looked toward the back door.

She hadn't exactly said that she was going to help him, but she was standing there, so what else could that mean?

He figured he'd better just ask.

"I...I don't want to make assumptions. You're here because you're taking the nanny job?"

"Yes. I said I would."

That was all he needed to hear. That warmed his heart and felt deep and right the same way her voice felt right on his ears.

"I have the beds ready," she said. "Do you want Kimbi on the top or bottom bunk?"

"Is there a railing?"

"Yes, but not to the complete end of the bed."

"I see. I should have checked before I left." He'd just glanced in the room, knew there were bunkbeds in there, but couldn't remember what they looked like. "How about let's put Hazel on the top bunk, just because I know I can lift her up. That'll save you, and then they can decide tomorrow which one gets which."

"Or they can both decide they want the same one," Willan said, with humor lacing her tone. She wasn't making fun of his kids. She was just saying that about kids in general.

"You said you never had children?"

"No."

"You sure know how they act."

"I suppose they act the same with the librarian as they do at home. There must be ten thousand books in the library, and they'll all fight over one."

"Yeah. That's exactly right."

He opened the back door, softly, and then met her eyes as she walked around him and bent in. She didn't seem pretentious, wasn't trying to impress anyone, and wasn't bragging about herself.

He could find a lot to admire in her.

He walked around to the other side, and by the time he had Hazel's door open, Willan had pulled Kimbi out.

She did it so gently Kimbi hardly groaned, and he had to say he was impressed.

When he reached in the other side and started picking Hazel up, she whined and then said, "Mommy? Where's Mommy? Nanny? I want Nanny."

"Shh, sweetheart. You're okay. Daddy's here."

"I want Nanny," Hazel said, more insistently this time.

"We'll talk about that tomorrow, but right now, I'm here with you. Put your arms around my neck."

She whined and cried a little, but her arms went around his neck as he lifted her up, careful not to bump her head as he pulled her out of the car.

He supposed he thought Willan would go in, but she was standing at the top of the stairs waiting on him.

"Can't you get the door?" he said, then kicked himself. Probably not. Hazel wasn't that heavy to him, but to Willan, who wasn't used to lifting anything heavier than a book, Kimbi probably weighed a ton, especially since she was older. He should have been the one carrying her.

"I think she has a fever," she said.

He stopped short. He'd never dealt with them when they were sick. Never dealt with them alone. There had always been someone who was knowledgeable about children to oversee them, someone he could talk to about them. His wife might not have been there, but whatever nanny they had at the time would have been.

"Should we drive her to the emergency room?" he said, having no idea of anything else they could do.

"Um, well, I was thinking we might want to take her temperature, maybe give her a little Tylenol or something. Her breathing sounds fine, she doesn't seem to be in any pain, and she's not groaning or coughing. I just think it's maybe a summer virus? Something she might have picked up on the plane or at the airport?"

"Okay. Let me get Hazel settled in bed, and you can take her to the kitchen, if you would, and sit down and wait on me?"

"Okay."

Hazel didn't want to let go of his neck when he set her in bed, and he laid his head down on the pillow beside her for a few minutes until she relaxed again. Thankfully, it had been a big day for her, and she was tired and drifted back off easily.

There had been so much upheaval in their short lives. In the last six months, things had gone crazy for them.

He wasn't even sure what all they'd been through with their mother, but he had his lawyers working on something that hopefully would give them some stability with him. Isla wasn't too interested in being a mom. He didn't think, especially right now, she'd fight him too much for custody.

Maybe it was selfish of him, but he wasn't looking at it like that. He just really wanted his daughters to have a stable home life.

He wished he could go back and do things over again. Because he'd really like them to have a mom and a dad and the support of a traditional family, just as he had.

He'd made a lot of movies since they'd been born, but he'd give them all up to give his kids the kind of life they needed in order to thrive.

Slipping away from Hazel, he tiptoed out of the room and walked through the living room into the dark kitchen. "You don't have to sit here in the dark."

"I was afraid if I turned on the light, it might wake her up. And she doesn't know me. She might be a little upset to wake up in the arms of a stranger."

"That makes sense," he said. And again, he appreciated the fact that she put the needs of his child ahead of her own. Not that sitting in the dark was such a sacrifice, but it was more of a sacrifice than some people would want to make. He'd certainly met people who thought life was all about them.

In the short time he'd known her, he'd figured out that Willan was humble and willing to give up her way.

"I know there's a thermometer in one of the bags in the car. I'm going to go grab them, and I'll be right back in."

"Take your time. She feels warm, and she's breathing a little bit fast, but her breathing is clear, and I think she's fine."

"Thanks."

When the flight nanny had handed him off the bags, she'd mentioned that the toiletries and other things were in one of them. The handheld one, she'd said.

Hopefully, that meant medicine as well as combs and brushes and toothpaste.

It took him about ten minutes, but he did find a thermometer as well as some fever medication.

He stuffed those in his back pocket and grabbed some bags to carry in.

Willan was right where he'd left her.

"I think this is one of those thermometers that you just aim at the forehead. I think I can reach her if you hold still."

"Okay."

He grabbed it out of the box and used the light from his phone to read the directions to make sure he was doing it right. Back when they were babies, he remembered taking a temperature a time or two, but it wasn't something he'd done on a regular basis, certainly not enough to be confident that he was doing it right.

He pressed the button, and the thermometer beeped after just a few seconds.

The display read 102.1.

"You're right. She does have a fever. Let me read how much her dosage should be and I'll get her some medicine."

Kimbi stirred, fussing, and Willan started humming and rocking her, like she had children all her life. He did think that maybe handling children came a little more instinctively to women than to men, at least it had in his experience, but Willan seemed to be a natural.

"Thankfully, this is liquid. But we're going to have to wake her up enough to get her to swallow it. Do you mind holding her? I'll try to make sure that she sees me. I'll turn on the light over the stove so we have a little bit of illumination, but nothing bright that's going to irritate her."

"I'll go along with whatever you do."

It was nice that she didn't have sixteen different better ways to do things and could just follow along with him.

That was certainly a welcome change.

Not that he had to be the leader all the time, but when someone was taking charge and doing their best to make something good out of a bad situation, it was annoying when someone who hadn't been willing to take charge to begin with all of the sudden felt like they needed to voice their better ideas, even if they didn't want to lead.

He shoved those thoughts aside. He seemed to be seeing all the good qualities in Willan. Probably because she was helping with his children, maybe because he'd just been around some bad apples.

She wasn't any different than anyone else, and he needed to remember that.

Especially if she was going to be working as his nanny.

His wife had already run off with a nanny. He didn't need to follow in her footsteps.

"Kimbi, honey," he said as he scrunched down beside her, the correct dosage of medicine in the little cup in his hand. "Kimbi? Wake up, sweetheart, and swallow this. It tastes like bubblegum."

She groaned and fussed a little, and her eyes cracked. "Daddy?"

"That's right, baby. It's Daddy. I have some medicine for you to take. You're gonna love it. It tastes like bubblegum."

Her lips cracked open, and she said, "I want to lie down."

"You swallow this, and then we'll get you all tucked in bed, okay?"

She nodded, tilting her head back and draining the little cup.

"That was a little easier than what I was expecting it to be," he said under his breath, meeting Willan's eyes as he straightened.

"Me too. I've heard so many horror stories about children not wanting to take their medicine."

"The bubblegum taste helps." That, and the fact that maybe his daughter felt safe in Willan's arms. Or maybe she just was happy to be with her dad.

"I can carry her, if you want."

"She might go down easier with you," Willan said as she shifted, adjusting Kimbi so that it was easier for him to get his arms underneath her.

"If you hold on a second, I'd like to talk to you."

"Okay."

He lifted his daughter and couldn't help but smile as she snuggled deeper into his arms, although a thread of worry went through him.

Hopefully, Willan was right and it was just a summer virus. He didn't want to think that it was anything serious.

Regardless, Willan had definitely proven to him tonight, not just because of feeling his daughter and knowing she felt warmer than normal but with taking care of her and being more interested in his kids than she was in trying to impress him, that she was the person he wanted to help him with the kids.

He just needed to work out what that was going to look like.

Chapter 7

Maybe she should have stayed in the kitchen, but Willan felt claustrophobic in the small dark, unfamiliar house.

So she went outside and sat on the porch steps where she'd been when she'd first seen his headlights coming over the rise.

It was barely five minutes later when she heard the screen door squeak and footsteps on the porch.

"I didn't think I saw you in the kitchen. But it's kind of dark."

"I'm sorry. I could have texted you where I was going to be." They had exchanged phone numbers before he left to get the kids. That's how she knew approximately what time he was going to be home.

Probably he didn't think a text was the best way to discuss job expectations, though.

She appreciated that. Although having things in writing was never a bad idea.

Despite the fact that Drake was a product of Hollywood, she didn't think that he would lie to her. Or anyone. So far anyway, he'd seemed so much more down to earth and honest than the stereotypical Hollywood actor would have her believe.

Really, she didn't want to believe that he was a famous movie star.

That just meant he was so much more out of her reach.

Not that she'd set her sights on him, but...she had thought there was potential to have something between them.

Obviously, she and a million other women, knowing now what he was.

"The house isn't that big. I found you without too much trouble." The door closed softly behind him, and he walked over, leaning against the opposite porch post.

"I've been to Chicago, plenty of times, and I've admired Lake Michigan from high-rise hotels downtown, but... There's just something about feeling the breeze on your face, and smelling that air, and breathing it deep, that makes the view from the high-rise not nearly as real and rich."

"I wouldn't know." She didn't mean that in a pity me kind of way, but there was no point in them talking about stuff like that; she couldn't hold up her end of the conversation. She had no idea what Lake Michigan looked like from an expensive high-rise hotel. "I suppose the more of the senses that you get into the experience, the richer and deeper and more meaningful the experiences," she said, realizing her last statement had been rather short, and she didn't want him to get the wrong idea. She didn't wish, not for one second, that she had an expensive view of Lake Michigan.

What she could see from the Indigo Inn was all she needed.

"Sometimes, it's good to get out of your bubble and see things from a different perspective. No matter what your perspective is to begin with, it never hurts to look at things through someone else's view."

"I can't disagree with that," she said, thinking about all the books she'd read over the years. That was kind of like looking at things through someone else's point of view, when you read a book written by a stranger, and you jumped into the world that they created.

Or, even better, the biographies and autobiographies that she'd read over the years.

"I guess I haven't done much living. Actual experience living," she said eventually.

"I guess I've had a lot of experiences, but they all come from the same bubble. Same people around me, everyone thinking the same things, all of us knowing for sure that we're right and having righteous derision for the people who disagree with us." His tone seemed to hold a little derision for himself, although she wasn't sure whether it was righteous or not.

"That sounds sad."

"It is. You lose touch with everyone but people who agree with you, people who love you or who love what you can do for them, and you forget that there are other people who completely disagree with you, good people, and that doesn't make them evil. It just makes them different."

"Right. We have a tendency to divide people because of their skin color, or their race, or where they're from, but it's really experiences that make people different."

"It's how we handle those experiences, our reactions and responses, that either create our character or show the lack. That's the true worth of the person. Their character."

"Deep thoughts," she said, wanting to lighten the mood some. She wasn't sure she wanted to talk philosophy, psychology, or the combination of the two of them or whatever he was trying to get at.

"I guess."

"If you're saying that you want someone more diverse than me to watch your children, you can just say so. We don't have to have a long and involved discussion of all the things I lack before you get to your point."

Why was she so defensive? He hadn't implied that she wasn't good enough, not in any way. It was just her feeling that way. Her insecurities coming out. Her perfectionist tendencies, knowing that she would never be the kind of woman he was used to being with.

"I didn't mean that at all. How did you get that?" he asked, truly sounding puzzled.

"I'm sorry. That's the worst part of me that just came out."

"I guess we all have a part like that, don't we? That part that we're working on, that we keep thinking is going to get better, and yet somehow we take a couple steps forward and look up only to find out we just walked in a circle."

She laughed. "You just described my life."

"Mine too. I feel like this is the elephant in the room, but I guess you know I'm hiding out here at Indigo Inn to get away from all the gossip and recover." He let out a breath and shifted, running a hand through his hair like he was uncomfortable. "Not very manly for me to admit that I need to recover, but I guess that's it. You know my wife ran off with the nanny.

That was more than a little embarrassing. The fact that I—this big movie star—couldn't keep her, wasn't enough, that not only did she find someone better, but she obviously never really liked me that much to begin with, since her preferences run toward women." By the time he was done, bitterness was evident in every syllable.

"You know it's funny how the things that we're concerned about, the things that we worry about, the things we're thinking about aren't the things that other people are worried or concerned about or even notice. I honestly hadn't been paying attention to any of the Hollywood gossip lately. I had no idea."

Maybe that explained why he was giving her odd looks and why he had hesitated to take her up on the nanny offer.

She couldn't remember if he'd seemed overly suspicious or not. Since she'd been completely clueless, she hadn't been able to reassure him. But she could now.

"I definitely recognized your name. I didn't recognize you at first though. That beard."

"No. It's a great disguise. Especially with a ball cap. I've never had a role where I wore one on the big screen before. But the painter duds help too. People aren't expecting to see me walking around actually holding a paint can and a paintbrush and using it."

She smiled, knowing that was true. Nobody really gave a flip whether she was carrying a paintbrush around and using it or not.

What different lives they had.

"Was that why you were telling me about different perspectives and different lives? Just to emphasize the differences between us?"

"No. I guess not. It's something I've been thinking about since I came here. So many times, the people I work with don't realize there's a life outside of what they do. But I suppose that's true of everyone. I'm guilty of that, just as much as anyone. I guess. It has nothing to do with you. I didn't mean to make it sound like it did."

"You didn't. Not until the end there, where I guess my suspicions took over, and that was me, not you."

"I've heard that line before," he said, a little bit of tease in his tone.

She glanced over and grinned at him, the light from the stars illuminating the grin on his own face. Funny that he was a big movie star, but she felt comfortable with him. Not comfortable with the idea of him, but comfortable with the actual man of him.

"I don't want to keep you up. Tomorrow is likely to be a big day with the girls, and I was going to stay home from work to try to make things smoother if that's okay. They know me and are used to me, although I haven't seen them for more than a month. But I thought the transition would go easier if I'm around for a day before I leave you alone with them. It's not that I don't trust you."

"No, that's fine."

He continued like she hadn't spoken. "I've gotten to know Leiklyn and Ethan pretty well, and any friend of theirs is a friend of mine."

"I guess that makes us friends, since Leiklyn and I've been friends since high school. We lost touch for a while, but I think working on the inn together will be really good for both of us."

"You guys are doing a great thing with the inn. It's a wonderful building, and you're hitting it at just the right time, with the new hospital going in and Blueberry Beach expanding." His voice trailed off. "I hate to see it lose its small-town charm though. It's a really special place."

"You know, I grew up here. But I needed to move away and make a lot of mistakes before I could come back and see that what you just said is absolutely true."

They sat in silence for a little bit, a breeze blowing softly, and the relaxing sound of waves hitting the beach rhythmic in the background, before he stirred himself. "I keep saying I want to keep you, then I don't say what I came out here to say. We never talked about your salary, or how many hours you're going to work, or your expectations."

She lifted her hands. "I don't have any. I worked as a librarian. Never a nanny. But getting the inn done is pretty important." She took a breath to steady herself. She didn't really mean to, but her chin jutted out, almost as though she were expecting a blow to it. "I assume that you're not going to be here long."

He was a Hollywood movie star; of course he wasn't staying long.

"No. I would say by the end of the year, the entire inn should be done, as long as money isn't an issue."

"It's not. Not anymore." She didn't say anything else, uncertain whether he'd heard that it was her inheritance that was going to be footing the bill for now.

"I'm not taking any payment, not now, and I'm not planning on it, I just needed something to do to keep my mind off of everything that was going on in my life. But yeah, this is just a temporary position. At the very most, it'll all be done by Christmas, and I'll be heading out. I was able to cancel one project and delay another one, but that's all the time I can spend."

"If you stay away from Hollywood too long, people forget you."

"That's the truth."

"Probably more true for women than men though," she said. It wasn't a sexist thing, not really. It was just the truth. Men seemed to look better as they aged, women...didn't.

"It's not fair, but then again, life really isn't." He shoved a hand in his pocket and looked down at her. "You think you have six months to help me out with the girls?"

"I do. I said I would, and I meant it. However long it takes."

They stood there in silence for a while, looking out across the dark waters of Lake Michigan, as the breeze ruffled across their skin and through their hair and rustled the grass as it passed.

Finally, he looked over at her again. "I've never been in charge of hiring the nanny before, but as I recall, they're on call at night if there's any kind of emergency, but they have some guaranteed hours off in the evening and one guaranteed day every week off. I can work whatever days I want to at the inn, so you can pick any day you'd like to have off. And you're right. It's just a temporary thing, so you can expect work until Christmas. If you need to help at the inn or do anything for yourself, and the kids are in the way, we can find someone else to help them part-time."

He named a figure. A weekly salary that was more than she made in a month at the library. Hearing that number should make her happy, but it actually made her want to jump up and run.

It wasn't that she couldn't spend that kind of money, because she could. Not just on the inn. She could buy a house, get a car, give money away, afford the plastic surgery that she'd always thought she needed in order to look good. She could look as good as money could buy, getting paid that amount.

It wasn't the amount that upset her. It was the idea that those kinds of numbers didn't even faze him. It didn't even sound like a lot to him—that's what he paid the nanny, just a pittance. It showcased the gulf between them, and what had felt like a warm and cozy conversation had taken a turn to cold and unfeeling.

It made her acutely aware that she had absolutely nothing in common with this man. He was just being nice to her, stooping down, bending over, and giving her a little of his very valuable time.

Chapter 8

"If that's not enough, I could double it," Drake finally said when minutes ticked by and Willan hadn't answered him.

It was on the tip of her tongue to deny him, but why? If he was going to pay her double, why would she turn it down?

Because it was insane to get paid that kind of money to take care of children. Absolutely insane.

"Your children are very valuable," she finally said, knowing that didn't answer any questions at all, didn't even really have anything to do with the conversation they were having, but she couldn't get anything else out. She'd never been floored by a job offer, by a money offer, like she just was.

"I didn't think you were going to drive such a hard bargain. That's fine. I'll triple it."

She couldn't take it anymore; she jerked away from the post, turned around, and strode toward the door. She stopped short when she remembered it wasn't her house.

Turning back around, she stomped to the stairs before she stopped, still agitated, moving her hands, wanting to rake them through her hair and yell at the universe for some reason. Just couldn't handle the irritation that bubbled up inside her.

Irritation about what? There wasn't anything to be irritated about. She should be jubilant.

"What's the problem?" He sounded truly baffled. He probably really didn't know.

"When you first came to Hollywood, the first role that you had in a movie? Was it a big one?"

"I'm one of the lucky ones. I was actually chosen to be in a movie with a lot of buzz." He named the movie, and it was one even she recognized. "It was a coveted position, and I landed it. Then I aced the part.

It was like it was made for me. After that, parts just fell into my lap. Why?"

"Do you remember what you were offered for that first film?"

"If you're trying to get me to offer you my starting salary—"

"No," she interrupted him. "I was just wondering if you remember how you felt when you first saw or heard the offer for the amount of money that you were going to make from that film."

"I was shocked. We were talking seven figures, and up until that point, I'd made like $20,000 a year working for my dad in construction. Couldn't believe I was going to work six weeks and make more than $1 million." He laughed a little. "Of course, I had another rude awakening when I realized that I was only going to keep about half of that million dollars, and the rest of it was going to go to various taxes."

She sighed. "I'll keep that in mind." She wasn't sure whether he was going to pay her taxes or if she was, but she didn't want to end up in jail over it, so she'd probably better figure something out.

But that really wasn't what she was thinking, and she said, "That's how I feel right now. What you offered me to begin with is more per week than I made in a month at the library. And then you just double it and then triple it without blinking an eye. I feel like I've stepped out of Kansas and into a different dimension."

"Well, maybe that's your problem, since we're not in Kansas. This is Michigan."

She laughed, as she was sure he had intended.

"I'm kidding. I understand what you're saying. And that's why it took you so long to respond. Man, I thought I was going to have to sell a kidney in order to keep you with my girls. After what I saw this evening, you impress me. Not sure I want anyone else watching them."

He almost sounded like he didn't want to say that. Like he was afraid to give her a compliment. Afraid she might read more into it than what he meant.

"I think I've told you several times now, I said I would do it. Even if you don't pay me, I'll do it."

"You would do it for free?"

She laughed. "Yeah. I did just inherit some money, but I think it's going to take most of that to fix the inn. But I don't care. I just..."

She wasn't sure whether she could tell him that she didn't like the direction her life was heading. She also didn't want him to get the idea that she was hinting around that he needed to do something to fix that or that she wanted to hang on his coattails somewhere. Just didn't want him to think that it had anything to do with him.

She wasn't sure why that was so important, but it was.

"You just what?" he prompted.

She didn't have much experience with men, but the little she had said that they were much more interested in talking about themselves than they were in listening to her talk about herself. But Drake sounded like he actually wanted to know.

Maybe he was just a good actor. She almost laughed at the thought but stopped herself in time. How could she explain that?

"I just said I would. So, whether you pay me or whether you don't, it doesn't matter. I'm here."

"It's been a long time since I've met someone like you."

"You say that like you used to know people like me," she said, finding that interesting, if not impossible.

"Not exactly like you, but where I grew up in rural Wisconsin, people were salt of the earth. Honest and hardworking, and willing to lend a hand no matter what."

"No wonder you like it here in Blueberry Beach so much."

"Yeah. It's just that small-town thing. I guess, sometimes towns lose that vibe when they grow too quickly. For now, I for sure feel it here in Blueberry Beach."

"You act like you miss it. Is Hollywood that important?"

"You know, I was thinking tonight that maybe I don't want this life for my girls. Maybe I want something a little sturdier for them. A little more traditional."

"We were just talking about how you need to be able to see other people's point of view. Isn't that the stereotype of small towns? That they can only see themselves and can't imagine the bigger world?"

"I was actually thinking the opposite. You get in the city, and you get that same bubble. People can only see themselves, they don't give a thought about anything besides the here and now, and they actually are kind of arrogant about how diverse and inclusive they are, when they're only diverse and inclusive with the right kind of people. They're rather moral and righteous about it. Sure, they live side by side with different cultures, but those cultures are still living in the same city they are, doing the same jobs, eating at the same places. There's more similarity than they think."

"There we are getting deep again," she said, not really wanting to go there. She wasn't sure exactly where she fell on that. She did know that she spent most of her life focused on herself. Which was probably even worse than being focused on the area that a person lived in.

"It's pretty late for that. You're right. How about I let you go to bed, and we'll see what the morning brings?"

"Of course. If you don't mind, I'm gonna check Kimbi before I go to bed."

"We can go in together. Because I was going to do the same thing."

As much as she loved standing outside, feeling the breeze, enjoying the night air, she was tired. Even though she'd never actually been a nanny, she knew that watching small children was not an easy thing, and tomorrow was likely to be a very tiring day.

He opened the door for her, and she walked in ahead of him, slipping softly into the girls' room and reaching out to touch Kimbi's forehead.

"She's much cooler," she whispered as she stood.

"That's fantastic," he said, and his voice held all the tones of relief. He bent down while she slipped out, but she waited for him to come out before going to her room.

He closed the girls' door softly behind him before he said, "I believe you're right. She felt a little sweaty. I always heard that that means a fever has broken."

"Yes." She'd heard the same thing.

"Thank you so much for noticing that she had one to begin with. I probably would not have noticed or just figured she was warm from sitting in the back of the car. I owe you."

"She might have been fine without the medicine. We'll watch her in the morning." She kind of brushed off his words, although they made her feel good.

She'd always known that she wasn't good enough to keep a man interested. She was imperfect. Too much chub around her belly, too many other problem areas to list, all those imperfections had always been her main focus, but somewhere, deep in the back of her mind, she'd also wondered if she was really cut out to be a mother anyway.

Maybe she didn't have what it took. Maybe she'd never ended up with a man because having a family was beyond her capabilities.

"You're in?" Drake said.

"Yes."

"Thanks. We'll go with the last number I gave you, okay?"

She laughed. "Whatever. I don't care. I just don't want to go to jail for not paying my taxes."

He laughed with her. "I'll try to help you out with that. I'll get you connected with my accountant. He's good."

"He's probably expensive."

"Now you can afford him."

"That's great. I can afford your accountant and have enough left over to buy cereal."

"You might have a little bit more than that left."

"Maybe it'd be good if I didn't. If I can't afford to buy food, maybe I'll actually lose the extra weight I seem to have carried around all my life."

"Extra weight? By Hollywood standards, maybe. I just think it's really nice not to be constantly surrounded with a walking skeleton. You're perfect the way you are."

She wished she could believe him.

Chapter 9

The next morning, Willan was up early.

She'd always been a morning person and didn't see any reason to stay in bed when she was ready to get up.

She'd already enjoyed a cup of coffee on the front porch, and although the sun rose behind her, the reflection on the water was still gorgeous.

There was something about early mornings that she loved, and she didn't miss them if she could help it.

Although, she'd spent eighteen years growing up in Blueberry Beach, and come about October, it'd be way too cold to be enjoying anything, and in January and February, the best place to be for anything would be snuggled up indoors.

Still, there was a certain appeal to that as well, although with children it might be different.

By January and February, Drake and his kids would be gone.

She was standing at the counter and had just put some toast in the toaster when a little voice behind her said, "You're not my mommy. You're not my nanny either. Who are you?"

She turned slowly and gave a little smile, not wanting to come on too strong. In her experience, and she had a lot of experience with children who didn't know her very well coming in and out of the library, children did better with adults they didn't know if those adults stayed back and gave them a little room to get used to them.

"I'm not. My name is Willan, and I'm a friend of your daddy's."

She wouldn't know whether he would classify their relationship as friends, exactly, or not. But she didn't know what else to call it, so she went with her gut.

Her gut also said that Drake wasn't going to argue with her. He wouldn't be a stickler and insist that he was her employer, that she needed to get the relationship right.

But she wanted to be able to say they were friends.

She didn't know why it was so important, but she vowed not to care.

However, telling herself not to care and actually being able to not care were typically two different things.

"I want my mommy," the little girl said, sticking her lip out. She crossed her arms over her chest.

Thinking back over her years of working with children, she noticed something in Hazel's eyes...

"Are you hungry?" She tried to sound sweet and nice.

Sure enough, Hazel's eyes flickered, and her lip moved, almost as though she were forgetting to hold it out in a pout. "I want cereal."

"Have you ever had cinnamon toast?"

The little girl nodded slowly. "But I like Super Sugar Ball cereal."

"No. I mean real cinnamon toast."

The toaster picked that moment to pop the toast up, as though emphasizing her words.

It was the first time in her life Willan thought a toaster had perfect timing.

Hazel's eyes got big, then her brows drew in, and she tried to look around Willan as though the answer to her questions might be on the counter or in the toaster.

"What's that?" she asked, taking a tiny step forward. The lip that had been stuck out in a pout went back to its normal spot.

"You can help me make it if you want to." Willan tilted her head and allowed her eyes to smile along with her mouth.

Hazel's eyes grew big, and her mouth opened in an O. "Really?"

Willan nodded. "You can go ahead. Stand right here on this chair." She pulled a chair over and held her hands out to Hazel.

Hazel barely paused before she padded across the kitchen floor, grabbing Willan's hand and climbing up in the chair.

"I always wanted to help cook, but Mommy always told me no, she didn't have time and Nanny said I made too much of a mess. I want to be a cook when I grow up. On TV. Mommy watches shows like that all the time. She says that I have to learn to stop talking and listen before I can be a chef, but sometimes I have things to say, and nobody listens to me, and I wish they would because I think that I can learn to be a chef even if I can't always learn to be quiet. Do you mind if I talk? Because sometimes people say I talk too much, and I try not to, but I really want to help. And do a good job. And I don't want to be annoying because sometimes Mommy says I'm annoying too. Nanny never says I'm annoying, but sometimes I think she thinks I am. At least Kimbi says I'm annoying, but she's my sister and Nanny says sisters always think that other sisters are annoying, especially little sisters."

Willan was nodding and smiling as the little girl spoke. Such a cute little thing and starved for attention.

As soon as Hazel stopped to breathe, Willan said, "Can you put the butter on?"

"You're going to let me use a knife?" Her words were filled with astonishment.

"Will you be careful?" Willan asked, eyes narrowed just a little bit like she was conspiring with Hazel.

Hazel was very serious about making the toast, although she chattered the whole time. Willan helped her sprinkle just a little sugar and even less cinnamon over the top of the butter that they spread.

She sat down and ate the whole two pieces, surprising Willan by not even asking to have the crust cut off.

She barely popped the last piece of toast into her mouth when she eagerly asked, "Can we make two more pieces? I'm still hungry."

Willan wasn't sure whether she was actually still hungry, or if she just really loved to help.

"We sure can. And I bet when Daddy gets up, he'll let you make a couple of pieces for him. And maybe, if Kimbi feels better, she'll let you make some for her too."

"No. She'll want to make her own. But Daddy might let me. And you? Would you like toast?"

Willan nodded. "You know you just ate my two pieces of toast, and I didn't even realize it."

Hazel giggled, and Willan helped her back up in the chair. They had two more pieces made, and they were making Willan's pieces so they could eat together, when Willan turned and Kimbi was standing in the doorway.

Her instinct was to go over and put her hand on her forehead to see if her fever had come down, but Hazel would probably resist being touched by a person she didn't know.

Hopefully, Kimbi would be as easy to win over as Hazel had been.

"Good morning, sweetheart. I'm Willan." She stayed where she was, noting that Kimbi's cheeks were not flushed, nor were her eyes droopy, both signs she'd seen from children in the library whose parents hadn't realized they were sick when they sent them for story time.

"Who are you?" Kimbi asked as though Willan hadn't said anything.

"This is Miss Willan, and she's gonna be our new nanny. She's Daddy's friend."

That didn't really help Kimbi, because her eyes narrowed even further. "Daddy's friend?" She gave Willan a disdainful look that, up until that point, Willan had only seen adults give to each other. "You don't look like a movie star."

There was definitely a lot of snob in her voice. Maybe she'd misheard Drake when he said that she was only seven. She sounded like she was about seventeen.

"That's because I'm not. Who would want to watch me do anything on TV?"

"Movies are in theaters. TV is a completely different media," the little girl said, the snob, if possible, even more pronounced in her voice.

"I'm sorry. See? I know nothing about it. So movies, TV, anything that has to do with Hollywood and beautiful people, count me out."

Kimbi's words hurt Willan's heart more than she wanted to admit. That had been her stumbling block all of her life. She wasn't beautiful. She wasn't movie-star thin. Her skin was blotchy, her hair never did what it was supposed to, plus it was just gray brown.

Still, Willan's words were true, too. She found she really didn't care, because being a part of Hollywood had never been something she wanted with her life.

Being beautiful enough for some man to want to be with her had been.

But she'd left that goal behind. She was turning over a new leaf, starting the rest of her life, not worrying about being perfect, just concentrating on doing right and being the best person that she could be. Kind. Compassionate, thoughtful. Maybe even a little funny at times.

Surely, she could find a sense of humor in there somewhere.

She enjoyed being around people who made her laugh. Last night, she had enjoyed listening to Drake laugh the few times she'd said something a little bit funny.

She'd much rather make people laugh than bore them with her complaints or her narcissistic comments.

"What is she doing?" Kimbi nodded her head at Hazel.

"I'm making cinnamon toast. It's really good. And I bet I'm really good at making it. And Miss Willan said I could make you toast if you want me to." Hazel sounded and looked so eager Willan's heart went out to her.

She decided whatever they were going to have for lunch, Hazel would help her make it. In fact, every time she cooked anything in the kitchen, she would make sure Hazel was helping. Even if that meant there would be a slightly bigger mess. She looked at the grains of sugar and the specks of cinnamon all over the counter.

The mess didn't matter when it came with the smile of a child.

"Maybe I want to make my own," Kimbi said, lifting her head and almost looking down her nose at the counter where the toast was.

"I told you," Hazel said, looking at Willan.

"You sure did. But you wanted to make your own, so it makes sense that Kimbi would want to make hers, right? And you can make your dad's. Maybe he'll eat four slices and Kimbi can make two of them."

"And if you eat four slices, can we each make two of yours too?" Hazel asked, jumping on the idea that Kimbi needed the practice just as much as she did.

Willan loved her sweet heart, and she impulsively reached over and gave her a hug.

If she'd been thinking, she never would have done it, but she didn't need to worry, because Hazel didn't hesitate, leaning into her and wrapping her arms around her neck.

"You're the best nanny I've ever had. And you're the only one that lets me cook. I love you."

How could anyone resist such sweetness?

"I see that my daughter has fallen in love with you already this morning," Drake said from the kitchen doorway.

Willan lifted her eyes, probably all the adoration she felt for the little girl shining in them. She couldn't fall in love with these children. They were leaving. She was losing them. Just because they filled that hole in her heart that she'd had for such a long time, the longing and desire for children, didn't mean she got them.

She could like them, but she couldn't fall in love, because they would take her heart and it would hurt painfully when they left.

She had to keep reminding herself of that.

Chapter 10

As Willan turned, she saw Drake's hand on Kimbi's shoulder.

"I think Kimbi must be feeling better. Her face isn't flushed, but I haven't touched her forehead because I thought she might not like it since she doesn't really know me."

"I take it she hasn't been up as long as Hazel has. Give her a few more minutes. Apparently, you have some kind of child magic."

"No. I just have a willingness to clean up messes and a special affinity for little girls who are eager to help." She shared a special look with Hazel, who was grinning up at her.

"I see," Drake said as he moved his hand from Kimbi's shoulder to her forehead. "Feels cool. But I'm not a very good judge of this. Do you mind if Miss Willan touches it? She's the one who noticed last night that you were sick."

"I thought I remembered you telling me to drink something. Something that tasted like bubblegum."

"That's right. It was medicine to bring your fever down. You must have caught a bug or something on the plane, but it looks like you're doing better." As Drake spoke, he jerked his chin at Willan, asking her to come over quietly without saying anything.

Willan pulled her arms from around Hazel and slipped away, whispering to her to be careful not to fall off the chair.

She walked a few steps to Kimbi. "How about you put your hand on my forehead and see if I have a fever. And I'll put my hand on yours to see if you do." As a point of reference, she touched her own forehead for a second first just so she could compare how Kimbi's forehead felt.

Kimbi glanced up at her dad, who nodded, before she said, "Okay."

It seemed to make her feel good that she could touch Willan's forehead, and she lifted her hand up without hesitation.

Just as Willan thought, Kimbi was as cool as she was, even slightly cooler. "She feels great." She smiled at Kimbi. "How do I feel?"

"You're a little warm. Maybe you should take some medicine."

"I don't think my medicine tastes quite as good as yours does. In fact, I think I have to swallow a pill, so unless I'm really sick, I'll probably not do it."

"Yeah. I think I was too sleepy to really taste it good. Maybe I should get more just in case I'm still sick. Right, Daddy?"

Drake grinned at his little girl. "I think I heard something about cinnamon toast. Like real cinnamon toast? I think that's better than bubblegum medicine any day."

"It smells good anyway," Kimbi said, her eyes drawn back over to the toaster, where Hazel had gotten tired of waiting and was sticking the spoon into the bowl of sugar.

"Remember what I told you, Hazel," Willan said as she walked across the kitchen, not wanting to grab the spoon from her but also not wanting her to dump an entire teaspoonful of sugar on one piece of toast. That would be a little bit too much.

Hazel dutifully knocked most of the sugar off the teaspoon and held up the little bit that was left. "This much?"

"That's perfect," Willan said, pushing the plate with the toast on it over a little so it was right under her spoon.

She finished helping Hazel make her toast, then Kimbi came over, insisting that she was too big to stand on a chair, so she stood on the floor while Willan gave her a hand. It wasn't long before they had enough toast for everyone to sit down to breakfast.

It surprised her that Drake said grace. If she'd thought about it, she would have assumed he wouldn't have, but that was her being judgmental.

Still, maybe there was a little bit of surprise on her face when he lifted his head. His brow raised, as though questioning what her look was for. She shrugged, the corners of her lips turning up.

There was something else in his eyes. She wasn't sure exactly what it was, maybe admiration?

That hardly seemed possible, but it's what she'd say if she saw that look on someone else's face. But the idea that someone like Drake would admire someone like her was kind of preposterous except...maybe he just appreciated that she had managed to make both of his girls forget about missing their mom and their nanny and excited about cooking breakfast.

As they looked at each other across the table, Hazel was still chattering away, talking about cinnamon toast and basically repeating every single thing that Willan had said that morning.

"Can't you be quiet for even one second?" Kimbi finally said, interrupting Hazel's monologue about how when a person makes cinnamon toast, they have to be so very careful not to dump an entire teaspoon of sugar on one piece of toast. It was the third time she'd mentioned it since they sat down to eat.

Immediately, Hazel's mouth snapped shut, and her eyes went to her plate.

This was the kind of thing that made Willan glad she wasn't a mom.

Hazel needed to learn that she couldn't monopolize every conversation.

But Kimbi needed to learn that she could be nice to people, even when they were annoying.

She wasn't sure what to do.

"I think you could have said that a little nicer, Kimbi," Drake said, giving his daughter a stern look.

Kimbi nodded and lowered her eyes.

"I know it's hard, Hazel, but sometimes we have to let other people talk too." Drake looked at his little girl until she lifted her eyes to his.

"I try. But sometimes I forget. Sometimes I just have words that I need to say, and they won't stop coming out of my mouth, and I just feel like I'm going to burst if I don't say everything." Her lip trembled, and she looked like she was going to cry.

"I don't think you're going to burst," Drake said. "Although, if I'm wrong, it could be kind of messy."

Willan supposed she should not have found that funny, but she snorted anyway. She hadn't quite gotten her mouth under control, and her teeth were definitely poking out in a smile when her eyes met Drake's across the table.

"I'm glad someone found my humor funny," he said kind of low and definitely meant for her ears.

"I thought it was funny too," Kimbi said, although she hadn't understood the implication of his comment and just wanted to be included with the adults.

"I didn't realize how funny your father was," Willan said, smiling a little at Kimbi and deciding not to call her out on the fact that she had no clue what was so funny.

"What do you guys think we ought to do today?" Drake asked, and they had a discussion with Drake insisting that they needed to do something that involved cooking in the kitchen, since both the girls really seemed to like it.

They finally decided they would go to one of the many blueberry stands around town, buy enough blueberries to make pies, come back, and make some pies and give them to the Indigo Inn and the Blueberry Café. Even though they couldn't sell them, they could offer people free pie. The girls practically levitated off their chairs over that idea.

"And Ruffles will get to see the kittens!" Hazel said. "Didn't you say she missed them?"

"I think she does," Willan said, looking at Ruffles's sad face as she lay on the floor.

"I think I'd like to hear about the kittens. Can we have kittens?" Kimbi seemed to forget for a moment that she was trying to present herself as a miniature adult and almost looked like a child with all the eagerness that any normal kid has when they start thinking about kittens.

"There are kittens at the inn!" Hazel said, like she knew where and what the inn was.

"The inn?" Kimbi looked around. "Is this an inn?"

"No, hon. This is a beach house. I've been working at the inn, fixing things up and getting rooms ready for people to stay in."

"But you make movies. Is there a movie at the inn?" Kimbi's eyes scrunched together as she tried to make sense of what her dad was doing.

Willan smiled to herself as Drake spent the next twenty minutes trying to explain to his girls why he wasn't making movies without actually telling them why he wasn't making movies. He also explained to them what he actually was doing, which shocked their socks off when they found out that their dad could do a real job working with his hands.

It was so sweet to see the girls treating their dad like a dad while knowing exactly what he did for a living.

They seemed so...normal.

After the girls got up and helped Willan clear the table, Drake sent them to change while he walked over to where she was wiping the counter around the toaster.

"You were pretty amazing with them this morning. Thank you. I had no idea they had wanted to cook so badly. I also didn't realize that people had told them they couldn't help."

"I don't think it hurts kids to hear no. But if you expect them to grow up and be able to feed themselves, they have to learn to do it sometime. Although, teaching little kids to cook is extremely messy. I didn't do that too much in the library, but little kids can make a mess with pretty much anything."

"Yeah. I already knew that. It makes the work harder, but it also makes them feel...loved, I think, when they're included in what the adults are doing and not sent off to play little-kid stuff all the time."

Willan nodded. "For sure. I remember that about my own childhood. I always wanted to be included in what Mom was doing, and she never seemed to have time for me."

Willan tried to say that with a smile and not like she wanted pity, because she really didn't. Her childhood was a long time ago; she'd certainly recovered from it. She could get over anything. After all, she'd decided to completely turn her life around, and she was going to do it.

Kind of ironic that when she decided to stop needing to look perfect, God sent a movie star into her life.

"What are you smiling about?"

She shook her head. "You know, you are really good with the girls. It was almost surreal to think that you're such a big star, and so popular, and command millions of dollars to make a movie, and there you are sitting at the table talking to your kids about kittens and puppies and making blueberry pies. It was sweet."

She said the word sweet, and their eyes met. Her hand, which had been wiping off the sugar on the counter, stilled. Her breath caught.

Something seemed to shift in the air around them, and it felt heavy. Expectant even.

Her chest felt tight. It almost hurt to take a deep breath. But she did and moved her eyes away, looking at the counter and taking about three seconds to remember that she had been wiping it and needed to finish.

"As soon as I get done here, I want to change my own clothes, and then I'll be ready to go." Her voice sounded a little shaky to her ears, but there wasn't anything she could do about that.

Drake cleared his throat, and his voice also seemed a little wobbly as he said, "Sure. Of course. I, uh, I also wanted to talk to you about moving to the lake house that I bought. It's not that far away, but it will be a lot less cramped than this place. It needs to be furnished, and I didn't know if you and the girls might want to decorate it?"

She was holding the rag underneath the water, rinsing it out, watching what she was doing, thankfully, because he would have seen the absolute shock on her face.

He had said something before, but she hadn't really thought he was serious. She pretty much had herself under control as she looked up. "You want me to decorate your house?"

"Sure. You and the girls."

"You want me to decorate the house with a five- and seven-year-old? So you want mostly primary colors and probably a lot of pink?"

She tilted her head a little and tried to put humor on her face.

This was no big deal to him. He was simply asking her to do something with his girls, probably something that he would not enjoy and would hire someone to do if she said no.

Still, it seemed kind of intimate for her to be decorating his house.

Drake Jensen's house.

Talk about surreal.

"If you don't want to, that's fine. Just say no. You won't hurt my feelings if that's what you're worried about."

"Oh my goodness. No. Not at all. I would love to! I just... You really caught me off guard. I think the girls and I would have a lot of fun picking things out. And they probably would enjoy decorating their own rooms, and... Are you sure you want me to seriously pick out the stuff that you're going to have in your house?"

"Sure." He shrugged his shoulders. "Why not?"

"Well..." She laid the rag on the counter, stretching it out so it would dry and straightening the edges, kind of absentmindedly, while she tried to figure out how to say this.

Finally, she leaned a hip against the sink and crossed her arms over her chest.

"Someday you'll probably get married again. In the meantime, you might bring ladies to the house. It just seems a little bit weird that they would be in the house using the stuff that I picked out."

"How would that be any different than hiring an interior decorator to do it? They'd be using her stuff instead?"

"Okay," she said uncertainly. She could see a huge difference in that, but if he couldn't... Maybe it was just a woman thing. Still, she felt like she needed to say one more thing. "Your...girlfriend, or whoever, may not feel that way."

"You're saying this is something that matters to a woman but not to a man?"

"I guess." She bit her lip. "Yes."

"All right. If that becomes a problem, which I'm fairly certain that it won't, because I'm not going to marry anyone or be with anyone who's going to have an issue with that. I would rather not be with someone than be with someone who's going to be a drama queen about everything. So, just on the off chance that I bump my head and forget all the things I've learned over the years and decide to do the stupid stuff that I did when I was younger, I'll simply redecorate the house." He put his hands on the counter and leaned on it, facing her. "How does that sound?"

She laughed. "That sounds like something I would never have thought of, because I've never had millions of dollars at my disposal before. So, it stands to reason that you could come up with a solution that was completely out of my realm of imagination."

"Maybe you need to get a better imagination," he said, straightening as Hazel and Kimbi bounded into the room. "I think we're ready to go as soon as Willan changes her clothes."

"We need to hurry. I want to see the kittens. And Ruffles is sad. So we need to cheer her up. And the kittens will do that," Hazel said, skipping over to where Ruffles lay on the floor and bending down beside her, petting her gently the way Willan had showed her.

She was such a sweet little girl.

Willan's heart twisted as she reminded herself, yet again, that she couldn't fall in love with these girls. Couldn't bear to love them, because they were leaving. And this conversation that she just had with their father emphasized the fact that they lived in completely different worlds and they didn't have anything in common and probably never would.

Chapter 11

Drake smiled to himself as he walked in the back door of the Indigo Inn.

Willan, Hazel, Kimbi, and Myla were sitting around the box of kittens, petting Ruffles and laughing at the dog as she lay her muzzle on her forepaws and stared at the babies in the box.

His girls had already come up with several dozen names for each kitten, including but not limited to Shoe, Bottle, Sweetie, and Mittens.

Myla had been very gracious about them, and while she hadn't committed to any names, she hadn't vetoed any either.

Willan gazed at the girls with that benevolent kind of look that mothers everywhere had.

Only she wasn't a mother.

Funny how she treated his daughters more like they were actual daughters than his own wife had.

Made his chest ache, but he wasn't sure exactly why. Maybe just longing for his daughters to be loved.

Or maybe it was a desire for something else. Something elusive. Something that he hadn't been able to find in his life so far. Something that felt like it was right there, right within his grasp, if only he could wise up and see it.

He had never been accused of being wise.

How did one go about getting wisdom?

He seemed to recall some verse in his childhood talking about God and wisdom. Maybe that God gave wisdom liberally. That wisdom came from the Bible.

Maybe he should look it up. He wanted to be wise, for his daughters' sakes. He wanted to be a good example and somehow raise them right in a world that seemed to be so wrong.

He'd seen a lot of wrong in his time in Hollywood.

Of course, Hollywood didn't have a monopoly on wrong. It was everywhere. So much easier to do wrong than right. His girls would find that as well. The weight of being a father lay heavy on his shoulders, and he thought again of Willan, loving his girls, gently correcting them, teaching them good things. Taking time to show them not just how to cook but how to be a gracious and compassionate person. How to take time and give it to others and set the things that were easiest for yourself aside.

She didn't need to preach with words; she showed them with her life.

Showed him.

He wanted his life to be like that. Like a sermon without words. It was so much easier to swallow when you had an example in front of you than when you had someone hitting you over the head with rules and regulations and preaching.

The first, everyone loved, the second, he, at least, resisted almost vehemently.

He made it to the stairs and started up, hearing voices down the hall and following them to the fourth bedroom on the left.

Pushing the door open, he said, "Can I come in?"

Ethan and Leiklyn were soon to be married, and he didn't want to interrupt anything.

It wasn't Ethan and Leiklyn in the room when he walked in.

"Pastor Kane," he said, surprised. "I wasn't expecting to see you in here with Ethan." He nodded at his friend, who returned the nod.

Ethan stood on a ladder, holding up a sheet of drywall, while Pastor Kane also stood on a stepladder, using a drill to put screws into the sheet he held to the ceiling.

"Someone told me they were going to be shorthanded today. I figured I ought to come and give a hand. I've missed most of the workdays that they've had because they're typically on Saturday, which is a day I reserve to make visits and go over my sermon notes."

"That makes sense. I guess that explains why I didn't realize that you are a handyman."

"I think we all have to be to some extent, although my family happened to be drywallers growing up."

"You got away from your roots, becoming a preacher and everything," Drake said, thinking of his own life and how he got away from his blue-collar roots as well.

Something fell over Pastor Kane's face. Maybe there was a little more to his story than what it seemed.

But the look was gone almost as soon as it appeared, and Drake convinced himself that he was seeing things.

Or maybe imagining them.

"I guess I can take the week off then," he said, surprising himself by not being opposed to the idea.

Of course, he wanted to spend time with his daughters, whom he hadn't seen in almost a month, but the idea of spending time with Willan was also a draw.

She would be a good friend. Funny and sweet and obviously not afraid to go the extra mile if it would benefit someone, as evidenced this morning by her letting his daughters make their own cinnamon toast.

Somehow, he thought that might be a great memory that his daughters would remember decades from now.

He knew he sure would.

"No way. I can step in for a couple of days, but the church needs me. Although, I love this opportunity. I have a tendency to be sedentary, doing a lot of studying and praying, and being up and being active is a great way to get refreshed and rejuvenated."

"That's how I felt. Coming here, the only thing on my mind had been getting away from everything that was going on on social media and kind of hiding out. But there's just something about working with your hands that allows you to kick your brain into neutral and make yourself tired enough to sleep."

Both men laughed at that. Anyone who had lifted those heavy sheets of drywall and held them up on the ceiling for an entire day didn't have any trouble sleeping at night.

"So did you just come so that you could kind of taunt us that you had a day off, or did you need help with something?" Ethan finally said, coming down from the ladder now that there were enough screws to hold the big sheet in place and grabbing his own drill before going back up the ladder.

"Yeah, I just mostly wanted to rub it in that I was kicking back and taking it easy." The guys laughed, and then he continued, "I'm kidding. We decided to come get some blueberries, and Willan is going to help the girls make pies. We'll be back later hopefully to deliver them."

"I love that. Faith. In action," Pastor Kane said without missing a beat with his drill.

They laughed, and Drake leaned against the doorframe.

"You're right. I can see them not turning out almost easier than I can see them actually being something we can share with people. But hey, like you said. I've got faith."

"I suppose it's possible for you to mess up the piecrust, but as long as you've got sugar and not salt in with the blueberries in the filling, I don't care," Ethan said. "I can take a spoon and eat it just as easy as a fork. In fact, you don't even need a crust. Just throw some berries and some sugar in a pie plate and give it to me."

"I don't recall telling ya that you're getting any," Drake said to Ethan.

"Really? I give you all the easy jobs for the last four weeks you've been here, and this is what I get? No blueberry pie?"

"All the easy jobs? That's rich. I've been doing all the grunt work since I came. Every job you don't want to do, you shove it off on me. It's a wonder you haven't sent me out to dig up the septic tank yet."

"That's tomorrow. Bring a shovel."

Funny, the longer he stood there, the more Drake felt like he needed to go look for a drill and start helping, but he really didn't want to leave his girls.

So he said what he had come to say. "I'll be back tomorrow, but I would like to take at least a day off every week. Willan's going to be watching the girls, and I appreciate that, but I want to spend some time with them, too."

He deliberately did not mention spending time with Willan. He didn't need anyone reading more into that than what there was. Just a friendship, that maybe would be a little bit more for the summer and fall but could never turn into anything.

He didn't live here, and even though he'd bought a vacation home here, he wasn't going to stay. He'd come back and hang out for a few weeks every summer, but his place was in LA. He had movies he needed to film next year.

Willan had a one-third interest in the Indigo Inn. She wasn't going anywhere.

Plus, she would be out of place in LA. She was a small-town girl, and Blueberry Beach was where she belonged.

He tried to picture her in Hollywood and just couldn't.

Although, come to think of it, he was having a little bit of trouble picturing himself in Hollywood. Blueberry Beach seemed to do that to him. Sucked him in and didn't want to let him go.

It was going to have to. His livelihood was not here. As much as he was enjoying the work he'd grown up doing, he had commitments next year and a career he wasn't going to flush down the toilet just because he preferred to be somewhere else.

"If you need me, it won't be a problem for me to hang out here for a day or two every week for the next month or so," the pastor offered. "As long as it's not a weekend. I can't do those."

"Course not. But yeah, if you take Drake's place, it'll be like he didn't leave. That'll keep us on schedule. I'd appreciate it." Ethan finished putting the last screw in and lowered his drill, resting it on the top of the ladder.

"Me too," Drake said, then he remembered, "Don't you have someone coming to work for a week while you and Leiklyn take a honeymoon?"

"I do. Although I don't think we'll be gone a week. We just have a couple of days planned, and then it's back here. I couldn't talk her into more. She's pretty set on getting this inn fixed, even though with Willan coming around with her inheritance, the money squeeze that we've been feeling has eased a good bit."

"I can imagine. It's great that she was able to put so much in."

"Yeah, it really eased Leiklyn's mind. Actually, I hadn't realized how much it was stressing me. Now, it's just a matter of time until we have everything looking as good as new. We even have some outside maintenance scheduled, including siding and a new roof."

"You're still thinking by the end of the year to have the entire thing pretty much ready?"

"I think so. We'll probably still do some renovations next year, sink more money into it than what we're planning on. But yeah, we're all getting excited about it."

Would Willan resent having to watch his kids and not being a part of this? He'd have to make sure to ask her. But then, he thought about the cinnamon toast this morning, and he was willing to bet that wherever Willan went, she'd take his kids along too. And that couldn't be anything but good for them.

Still, it would be considerate of him to ask her about it.

"All right, you guys. I want to get out of your hair. I'll be back in to work tomorrow. We can work out what day you want to come."

They exchanged numbers. Pastor Kane said he'd text with the day that best suited his schedule next week, and Drake whistled as he walked down the stairs.

He'd have an entire day to spend with his girls and Willan. What would they love to do? He wanted to plan something really fantastic because he wanted to see them smile. All three of them.

Chapter 12

"So how are you feeling?" Willan asked Myla as they sat on the porch together on opposite sides of the box of kittens.

Leiklyn had come out and asked the girls if they wanted to go with her to gather eggs, and after staring at her like they thought maybe she was really asking them to go to the grocery store, and after Leiklyn explained that they were going to go get the eggs from the chickens, they were jumping around with excitement and had trotted across the yard with her.

"Tired," Myla said with a weary smile. "And fat. I hate feeling like this, like my stomach leads me wherever I go. But on the other hand," her voice got a little dreamy as she put her hand over her round belly, "it's so cool to feel the baby move. Like, I have to smile every time."

"I bet," Willan said, grateful that her voice didn't hold an ounce of envy. Honestly, she was happy for the smile that was on Myla's face. It had been a hard decision for her to keep the baby, and it looked like she'd fallen in love with it, which made Willan happy for her, even though it wasn't going to be easy, whatever she decided to do—keep it or give it up.

She'd spent a little time talking to Myla, and she felt like maybe she could ask what she'd decided, but she didn't. It felt too much like prying.

"You look like you are having a lot of fun with Hazel and Kimbi. You're good with kids," Myla said, her head tilted, as she looked at Willan as though trying to figure out what it was about her that made her good with them.

"It's kind of weird since I don't have any of my own, isn't it?" Willan said easily, figuring that's what she meant.

"Yeah, but I guess...they're not yours. You know? Like there's something special about your own child, that you don't really feel with other children, right?"

Willan kind of looked at her, unsure exactly what she was saying.

"Like, this baby isn't even born yet, but I love it so much I can hardly contain how I feel. And I've never felt like that with any kid before. Like, you know kids are kind of annoying at times, dirty, and, I don't know, they made me tired. But this baby, my baby, it's different. Everything I feel is completely different," she said, shaking her head like she just couldn't figure it out.

"I think you're right. God puts a fierce love in a mother's heart. A fierce sense of protectiveness. An almost overwhelming desire to have the very best for her child. I think sometimes we go overboard and we almost become possessed with making sure that our kids get everything that they want, and we end up ruining them, because it's good for children to suffer. It's just hard for a mother to watch."

"You don't even have your own kids. How did you figure that out?"

"I've seen a lot of children and their mothers go through the library. It's funny, because the mothers who hover around their children, keeping them from ever having anything happen to them, making sure that they get the very best toys and everything their little hearts desire, aren't necessarily the mothers whose children grow up to be well-adjusted and successful." She huffed out a breath. "Maybe successful isn't the word I was looking for. Children with character. There. That's what I'm trying to say. Kids who work hard, who don't quit when things get hard, who know the value of truth and honesty, those kinds of things. You have to have hardships in order to learn them."

"That sounds wise. I can totally see how moms could go overboard. My baby's not even born, and I'm constantly thinking about what the best thing is that I can do for her. Right now, mostly that's eating the right things and getting enough sleep. But I've even thought about what kind of school would be best for her, and if I keep her, I need to start saving for a college fund. Isn't that crazy? She's not even born, and I want her to have everything."

"That's not crazy. It's natural," Willan said, smiling a little. Knowing she was right. Happy that Myla seemed to feel that way.

"You know, you almost look like you love those little girls." Myla tilted her head, studying Willan, who realized she had a happy little grin on her face as she watched Hazel and Kimbi skipping along beside Leiklyn out in the chicken pen.

"You know, I've longed for a child of my own. A family. A husband." She added that last bit, even though it felt like she was exposing a little more of herself than she felt completely comfortable with. She sighed. "But it just didn't happen. And I realized, as the years go by, just lately, that it's my fault that it didn't happen. I wanted everything to be perfect."

She didn't need to go into all of that, but maybe Myla could learn a little from her mistake. "But life's not perfect. It's messy. We make bad decisions, our bodies aren't perfect, our skin's not perfect, our houses aren't perfect, and nothing is perfect. And we just have to live anyway. And be happy. *Choose* to be happy. And choose to make the best out of everything we have. I guess that's a lesson that God needed to teach me. He taught me by the longing he gave me for a child and family and making me realize that I can't wait until everything is perfect before I move forward. I have to just keep moving, choosing the best way that I can, and when I make a mistake, I don't go back to square one and start again, I learn from it and keep on going."

"Do you think you're going to have children someday?" Myla asked, and then she looked over across the yard at Hazel and Kimbi. "Are you gonna be a nanny now instead of a librarian?"

"I don't know," Willan said, then stopped herself. "No. I'm not going to be a nanny. Drake and I have already talked, and I'm done with this job at the end of December, if not sooner. Whenever he's done working on the inn."

She would not be sad about that. She would not. And she would not allow her heart to hurt, either.

"Children just might not be what I get in this life. But whatever God has for me, I need to be happy with today. You know?"

"Yeah. I hadn't thought about that, but you're right. Because really, it's not what we get in life, it's what we give. How we live. How we bless others and live for them. It's so easy to get caught up in everything else and think that other things are more important."

"Exactly. You're so much further ahead of me, figuring that out now at your age."

"I made a pretty big mistake, a pretty obvious mistake, not that my baby is a mistake, but I guess I failed at doing a lot of the things I wanted to do, and it will be a waste if I didn't learn from them. Right?"

"Absolutely."

The kittens meowed as Cheddar got up and stretched then hopped out of the box.

She stood beside Ruffles, and they sniffed noses, almost as though Cheddar were saying to Ruffles, "Keep an eye on them while I go grab a drink and a bite to eat and take care of a few things."

Cheddar, seemingly satisfied that Ruffles got the memo, walked regally off the porch and disappeared out of sight.

Ruffles whined a little and then inched closer to the box.

"So did you hear any names earlier that you thought you might want to keep?" Willan asked as they smiled together over the dog who obviously took her job as guardian very seriously.

"I actually thought that if the girls wanted a kitten or two, they could name their own, and when they're ready to leave their mom, they'll have the kitten that they named. It's kinda silly for me to name them when they're just going to go to other people, right?"

"I guess. That's unselfish of you. I always loved naming animals, not that we had that many."

"I got to name Cheddar."

Willan noticed that her hand rubbed absently over her stomach. Maybe she was thinking of names for her own child. But Willan didn't ask, because as far as she knew, Myla hadn't decided for sure that she was keeping her.

They chatted some more until Leiklyn came back with the kids, and Drake came down from upstairs, and they left to go get the blueberries.

What Willan had said about just living each day as she got it, and being happy in it, had been directed at herself as much as Myla.

She'd been so concerned about falling in love with the girls, and how much it was going to hurt to have to watch them leave, that she forgot that it was more important to enjoy the moment and let tomorrow take care of itself.

Chapter 13

"I just checked on them. They're both out like lights." Drake allowed the screen door to shut quietly behind him and joined Willan on the porch.

A cloudless night and what seemed like a billion stars twinkled and shone down with such intensity he felt like he could reach out and touch them.

A warm breeze blew off the lake, and he lifted his face to it.

"I could get used to this," he murmured softly.

Willan chuckled. She sat sideways at the top of the steps, her back leaning against the porch post, one foot bent in front of her, one foot resting on the second step.

Her head was back, and her eyes were closed. "I think I could too, although I also feel like I could sleep for about seven years straight, so maybe check with me in the morning. Sometimes I get a little incoherent when I get tired."

"I thought I was the only one. I'm exhausted. Who knew taking care of kids was so difficult?"

He really did feel more exhausted than he did when he did manual labor all day. He also felt a little lightheaded, but that might just be because of Willan. She seemed to have that effect on him. Hadn't gone away since he first saw her. Actually, it seemed to have gotten worse.

Or maybe he was getting sick.

"We didn't just take care of the children. We did make pies. They turned out pretty well."

They'd kept one for themselves, and Drake had to agree with her. "I think I ate half of it myself."

"Normally, that's the kind of comment that is an exaggeration, but in your case... You did." She said that dryly, without opening her eyes.

"Oops. Please don't tell anyone, and I better not let that become a habit. I can stay in shape if I'm working at the inn, but if I'm standing

85

in the kitchen making pies, I might not show up quite the way I need to for my next action flick."

"I'm not sure it's the making of the pies that's the problem," Willan said softly and just as dryly, although her tone was also laced with humor.

"You might be whispering, but I heard that," Drake said, teasing. She was right; he'd eaten way too much pie, but it'd been so good.

"Oops. Got to remember when I'm talking to myself, I need to say it softer."

They laughed, and then he said, "Seriously, I've never made blueberry pies before. Never even thought about it. But I had so much fun today, my girls had a blast, and I honestly can't imagine how the day could have been any better."

That wasn't entirely true. He could think of a couple of things that would have made the day better. A couple of stolen kisses when the kids weren't looking. A soft touch, a secret smile. Warm memories and sweet anticipation.

But they weren't things he should be thinking of. There was no permanence with Willan, although just being able to end the day sitting here talking to her made everything feel like maybe it should be.

"Different times we've had big bake sales to raise money for the library, and I've made my share of pies. Growing up in Blueberry Beach, I've pretty much made blueberry everything, so if you have any questions, I can help you out."

"As much as I would love to spend every day for the next year in the kitchen making delicious recipes, it's pretty important for my physical well-being that I get back to work. If I did that, my action flick days would be over in about two weeks."

She huffed.

He thought maybe she wasn't going to say anything more, and then so softly he could barely hear her, she said, "I doubt that. Regardless, it's really not the way you look that made it so much fun for me."

Her words made his heart do a somersault, and he held his breath a little, hoping she would say more.

But she was silent, and he wasn't sure what to say. Because it wasn't the way she looked that made the day so good for him, either.

There was the laughter. The fun. The fact that it was a good day even though not everything went well—Kimbi dropped an entire bag of flour on the floor, and it scattered everywhere, and instead of getting upset about it, Willan looked at the mess and then laughed.

It made everyone else laugh as well, and they had a bit of a flour fight, and what could have been a real mood crusher became something that made the day even more fun and memorable.

"You know I never told you, but the reason that Anitra at the diner was looking at you so oddly was because you didn't quite get all the flour out of your hair."

"Seriously? You let me go to town with flour in my hair?"

"I didn't notice it until we were standing there. I kept thinking that she was looking at you oddly, and then I realized it was because one side of your head looked gray."

"Nice. I'll never be able to hold my head up in town again. They'll think I'm on some kind of weird cleanser or something. Is there a flour diet?"

"I'm pretty sure when people go on a diet, flour is one of the things they cut out. Although I'd never considered that maybe if you don't eat it, you can satisfy your craving by washing your hair in it. That's probably zero calories."

"I've pretty much been on every diet known to man, and I've never read one thing about people washing their hair in flour. Nice try though."

"Every diet known to man?"

"And none of them worked for me, I guess I should add," she said, sounding rather annoyed.

She shifted, lifting her head up and swinging around until both feet were in front of her. She wrapped her arms around her stomach and leaned forward, her head up like she was looking at the stars, but he thought maybe the whole diet thing was upsetting to her.

"I guess I don't understand. You look fine to me. Good even." She looked better than good, but he didn't want to ruin the fun camaraderie of the day by crossing lines he shouldn't.

She didn't say anything, and he stood for a while debating. He wanted to.

He supposed, coming from Hollywood the way he had, he understood there were a lot of insecurities in people, women and men alike. A lot of pressure to look unnaturally good. To base a lot of their worth, and how they felt about themselves, on how they looked and how they compared to some arbitrary standard of beauty that someone else said.

Finally, he said, "I think you have a beautiful heart. A beautiful spirit. One that is selfless and giving, and that's more valuable than whatever somebody looks like on the outside. Outside beauty is pretty much something that no one can change, or at least you have to work with what you've been given. But the heart? That's beautiful, because it wasn't handed to you. It was something you had to cultivate."

"Most of my life, I didn't do a very good job of cultivating that."

"You're doing a good job now." He pushed off the post and sat down beside her. "I could agree with what you just said though. I guess, the idea that I might have my children myself, that I need to be a good influence on them, that it's up to me how they turn out, and they're going to look at what I do more than they're going to listen to what I say, has prompted me to decide it's something I need to work on. You've been a good example to me."

"Thanks." She turned her head and looked to him for a moment before turning back. Her arms didn't loosen from around her stomach, but it felt like she relaxed a little. "Wow! Look at the lights out there. I think they're on the lake."

"A boat, maybe? It's really lit up."

"Yes, a boat. Boy, it's pretty. I bet it's even more beautiful out there on it." Her words were almost dreamy.

"Really? You grew up in Blueberry Beach, and you've never been on the lake at night?"

"I was never on a boat," she said, then chuckled. "I can tell I shocked you," she said after a moment's pause. "I know. It's kind of crazy that I grew up right beside the lake, and I've never even been out on a boat. How is that possible, right?"

"I guess that says a lot about your family life."

"Probably more than I want it to. Let's just forget about it." She sighed. "I used to sit on the rise right there at Indigo Inn and watch the ships at night. They were so pretty, and I used to dream about what it would be like. To own a boat. To be out in the water, hear the waves lapping against the sides, see the stars shining down, feel that lake breeze, and not have any cares and worries."

"I think everybody has cares and worries. Even people who are out in the boat in the middle of the lake at night, although maybe being somewhere like that makes your cares and worries seem not so important."

"Or maybe you just forget about them for a while, because there are too many other things to enjoy. You can hardly enjoy something and be worried about other things at the same time, now can you?"

"Good point. Maybe that's why we distract ourselves with things. Because you really can only think about one thing at a time."

"True." She let out a little sigh. "Have you ever been out on a boat?"

"I have. I've taken several cruises actually. Big cruise ships. I've gone on some charter fishing trips as well. Gone dolphin watching, and I have a friend who owns a yacht. Several friends actually."

"I see," she said softly, and he wished he would have kept his mouth shut. He just pretty much emphasized all the differences between them. He might not have said it with words, but he basically said *I'm rich, and I hang out with rich people.*

And there she was, dreaming about boats.

"I grew up in Wisconsin, Land of Lakes, right? My dad had an old fishing boat, and sometimes in the summer if we got done with a job early, or sometimes in order to get us to work, he'd say, if we get finished with this room before dark, we'll take the boat out tonight."

"In the dark?" she asked, seeming to like that story much more than she liked hearing about his rich friends.

"Sometimes we'd stay until after dark. That wasn't really the point. I guess when I was a kid, I didn't appreciate the night sounds, the smells, the relaxing atmosphere. I wanted to catch fish."

"And did you?"

He grunted. "Sometimes. I was too impatient. Made too much noise. Most of the time, I'd fish for about fifteen minutes before I wanted to swim."

"Did you jump off the boat?"

"Sure. It was fun. My brothers and I would see who could dive out the furthest. We'd have competitions to see who could hold their breath the longest too."

"That sounds dangerous."

"It probably was. But at the time, we didn't think so, and Dad just kinda laughed, enjoying watching us. Because, even though he had his line in the water, once we jumped in, he probably lost all hope of actually catching any fish."

"Didn't your mom go with you?"

"No. I don't remember her ever going out on the boat. I suppose Dad took my sisters once in a while, but I don't remember them ever being with me either."

"So your family was one of those where the boys hung out with the dad and the girls hung out with the mom?"

"Not really. But when it came to the boat, yeah. I guess I should ask my sisters if they ever wanted to go on the boat but didn't get to. I never even thought about it. Kids. How selfish, right?"

"Yeah. We are." She shrugged, her words sounding tired. "I guess some of us never really grow out of that."

"How could you say that? You've been completely unselfish with my girls."

"I'm glad. But that's not really the way I've lived most of my life."

They'd already talked about it, and while he hardly believed it, he couldn't dispute it since he didn't know her.

They watched as the lights they had been looking at moved off toward the right, eventually disappearing beyond the horizon.

"I wanted to ask if it's okay with you if I'm working at the inn all the time and you're not. I was thinking about that today while I was talking with Ethan and Pastor Kane. I...I thought that maybe there were some things you want to do that I might be keeping you from if you're with my girls all the time."

"The best way that I can help with the inn is to watch your girls so that you can help with the inn," she said, humor back in her tone. And then her arms did loosen, and she straightened so she no longer curled into a ball.

"I just wanted to make sure."

"It's fine. If I want to go to the inn, they can come with me. Just like they helped today. They can help me there, or they can hang out with Myla or play with the chickens or the kittens." She shrugged. "We'll make something work."

Ruffles got up from where she'd been lying in the corner, and she came over and sat down between them.

He scratched between her ears. "You heard Willan say kittens didn't you, girl?" he said, only half joking.

Ruffles whined again.

"I think she might actually understand," Willan said, more than a little shock in her voice.

"She's a smart dog."

"I couldn't believe no one wanted her. I looked all over, searching for her owners. I asked around at shelters and all the vets in the area, I even put signs up on telephone poles, which I've never done before in my life. But nothing."

"Maybe the Lord just had her for you."

"I guess. Probably. I didn't want a dog, that's for sure. She was pretty scruffy and seemed scared of everything at first, but she's such a good dog."

"She is. She's great with the girls too. I was a little nervous, but it all turned out okay."

He felt a little dizziness come over him, and he dropped his hand back into his lap and took a deep breath.

They were quiet for a bit when finally Willan said, "I'm going to bed. I'm feeling a little tired and maybe like I might have a touch of whatever it was that Kimbi had last night."

"I just had a little dizzy spell. I never even thought that we might have caught the fever she had." He moved to get up, pausing for a second before he stood, just to make sure the dizziness was gone. "I think I'm going to bed too."

"Hopefully, it's only an overnight thing for both of us as well," Willan said as she put a careful hand on the banister before she stood.

He turned and took a step, feeling dizzy again and all of the sudden eager to get somewhere where he could sit down or, better yet, lie down.

He'd barely taken a step to the door, intending to open it for Willan, when she turned and stumbled.

He put an arm out to steady her, putting his other hand against the door to steady himself.

"Are you okay?"

"I had felt fine until you mentioned your dizzy spell. I guess I felt like I needed to have one too, just in sympathy or something."

"Sorry. I didn't realize dizzy spells were contagious like yawns."

"I didn't know that either. But I guess I'll try to remember it."

"I'll keep my arm around you, just because I'm still not feeling the sturdiest, and I don't think either one of us wants to pick the other off the floor."

"I agree," she said, and her arm slipped around his waist.

He might be burning up with fever. That could explain the shiver that went through him and the way his breath hitched and froze in his lungs, but probably not.

"Let's stop in the kitchen, and I'll take your temperature." Through her shirt, he could feel her heat. "I think you have one."

"You feel warm under my hand, even through your T-shirt. I think you have one as well." Her words were slightly weaker and seemed to come from the top of her throat, with the least amount of effort possible.

They wobbled together into the kitchen where he opened the cupboard and grabbed the thermometer that he'd used yesterday.

It just took a couple of seconds to point it at her forehead. "103.9. That's pretty high," he said, feeling weakness stealing over all of his limbs. His knees wanted to buckle.

Her hand came up and brushed his fingers as she took the thermometer from him and held it in front of his forehead.

"104.1. Wow. That seems kinda high."

"I don't think I have any medicine for adults here," he said.

"I didn't think to bring any, either."

"I guess we still have the bubblegum fever reducer I gave to Hazel."

"It's in my room."

They didn't need to say anything more to each other but turned with their arms still supporting each other and wobbled to her room.

He flicked the light on as they walked in, and she grabbed the medicine off the nightstand.

"I wasn't sure where to put it away, and I didn't think about it after we got up today. We were busy."

"I'm glad. I feel like I can barely stand up."

"Me too." She held the bottle up. "No dosages for adults. You get half, I get half?"

"Nothing like a good scientific dosage, nice and accurate."

"That's what I thought." She poured the cup full, and he drained it, then she filled it full again and drank her own cupful. They finished off the bottle, alternating one for him, one for her.

As she drained the last one, her hand came down but missed her nightstand, and the cup fell to the floor.

Neither of them bothered to stoop and pick it up.

"Thanks. I think we'll feel better in a bit." His words sounded like they were coming from somewhere far away.

They stood there, him thinking that he needed to do something, trying to remember what it was.

Then it hit him. He needed to take his arm from around her and walk to his own room. He moved to do that, twisting a little. She moved with him, and somehow they both ended up facedown across the bed.

"Sorry," he mumbled. Maybe there was some kind of sleep aid in the medicine, because all of the sudden he could barely keep his eyes open.

"My fault. Give me a minute and I'll help you up," she said, her words slurred.

"No. I'll help you. In a minute."

"Let's stay here and think about it. Maybe my brain will start working if I just let my body rest for a moment."

"Good thinking," he said.

He was pretty sure he fell asleep first, since he never heard her snore.

Chapter 14

"So it was a short-lived fever for the girls and me, but Drake was down for three days." Willan shrugged and grabbed a grape off the tray from the table in front of her.

Her friends and co-owners of the inn, Tiffany and Leiklyn, were sitting at the table with her.

Night had fallen outside. In the morning, Leiklyn would be standing in front of the preacher and getting married to the boy she'd fallen in love with decades ago.

"I heard he also had a stomach flu that went along with that," Leiklyn said, with a little grin.

Willan wasn't going to disclose that little tidbit, but it sounded like Drake already had since he'd gone back to work two days ago.

She grinned and shrugged.

"That's good to know," Tiffany said, taking a bite of an apple slice.

"What?" Willan asked, grabbing another grape.

"That movie stars get stomach sicknesses just like the rest of us mere mortals." She sounded a little sarcastic, but her smile was genuine, and Willan grinned along with her.

"You know, I guess I don't really know what it takes to be a successful actor."

"Good looks," Leiklyn interrupted her.

"Right." And Drake certainly has those. She actually thought he looked better with his beard than without, although as she understood it, he didn't get to say whether he had a beard in his movies or not. All of that stuff was choreographed for him down to his haircut. "But he's a person just like us. You know. Maybe some people let all that stuff go to their head, but he's just really...normal."

"Other than he's a gorgeous millionaire, millions of women are in love with him, and he makes bookoo bucks for a couple of months' worth of work. Yeah, other than all that, he is so normal," Tiffany said, her words totally sarcastic and her face a little goofy. "But it's obvious that you really like him, maybe even more than like him," she added, narrowing her eyes at Willan and lifting her brows.

"I do. Even though he was miserable while he was sick, he wasn't a jerk. He's never been a jerk. I just... I just didn't know that there were men like that in the world."

And he said that what she looked like didn't matter. Maybe he didn't really mean it, maybe he was just saying that because he didn't want to hurt her feelings, but he acted like it didn't matter.

The way he treated her had nothing to do with how she looked, and he didn't seem to see all the flaws that seemed so large when she looked at herself. Actually, they didn't look so large anymore, because in the last week, he'd been making her forget them.

"But that's all it is, friendship," she added, just so that her friends were clear. "He's leaving as soon as the inn is done or at the end of the year. Whichever comes first."

"Maybe he'll take you with him? You and the children seem to get along so well."

"I love Hazel and Kimbi." That was putting it mildly. They'd captured her heart, and she absolutely adored them.

"How did you get away from them tonight?"

"Drake is home. He's been taking afternoons off since he went back to work. I think he was so weak from his sickness that he just couldn't work a solid day, so he came home in the afternoon, then went back in the evening. Today was the first day he worked a full day, and he came home for supper and stayed. The girls were so excited," she added. She didn't say that the girls had begged her to stay, too.

It cracked her heart a little, because she thought they just wanted to have what seemed like a normal family almost. Like...like they wanted her to be the mom.

She loved her friends, but she'd almost canceled tonight, because she'd wanted to give them exactly what they wanted, and so help her, she was starting to want that too.

That was going to break her heart more than anything. Almost as much as losing the girls. Because she was starting to want things she knew she could never have.

"Wow. A man who is willing to spend time with his children? And he's also a movie star?" Tiffany shook her head in wonder, and there was no sarcasm at all in her words. "It really does seem too good to be true. None of my husbands have ever been the slightest bit interested in doing anything with their children, and most of them almost resented the fact that their other wives might ask them to keep them for a bit."

"All of your exes had children?" Leiklyn asked.

That was information Willan hadn't heard, either. They really had drifted apart, and there was so much of their lives that were unknowns.

"Yeah. I guess I should have known if they were married before they probably weren't a good bet, but...people could say that about me too. Since I've just gotten my divorce finalized from number three." Her words were deliberately flippant, but the sadness in her eyes was unmistakable. It wasn't the way she'd expected her life to turn out.

One of Willan's lips pulled back, and she covered Tiffany's hand with her own. "I know I don't understand, about the divorces and the marriages and all of that, but I know that my life hasn't turned out the way I was expecting either." She squeezed Tiffany's hand.

"I know. It sucks, doesn't it?" Tiffany said, her words a lot tougher than the hurt in her eyes would seem.

"But I decided that I wasn't going to let my life just happen to me anymore. I was going to take charge and become the person that I wanted to be, instead of sitting around and wishing that life would just magically get better. It doesn't happen that way. At least... Not for most of us," she said, thinking of Drake and the break that he had getting into Hollywood.

"Sometimes, I think we look at people and think they've just been lucky, but a lot of times, they've worked for those breaks, or they've worked to be where they were standing, and when we say luck," Leiklyn used air quotes around the word luck, "we don't see all the hard work that it took to get to where they were to be able to take advantage of the luck that happened to them." She did the air quotes around luck again. It was pretty obvious that Leiklyn didn't believe in luck.

"You don't think things just randomly happen to people?" Tiffany asked.

"No. Not at all. I mean, of course random things happen, but take Drake, for example. If he hadn't taken the initiative to go to Hollywood. If he hadn't taken the initiative to go to the audition. If he hadn't practiced being a good actor. If he hadn't made sure that he was wearing the right clothes, had his face shaved, or if he hadn't known the right people or developed the right contacts or whatever it was that helped him get that first role in that first movie, he wouldn't have had it."

"I guess I kinda see what you're saying, but not everyone's blessed with movie-star looks."

"And that's the luck that happened to him that he had nothing to do about. But there are plenty of good-looking people who aren't movie stars. And why not? Maybe it's because they didn't put the work into whatever it takes to be a movie star. Maybe they thought that movie stardom was just going to land in their lap and all they had to do was smile and look pretty."

"That's exactly right, Leiklyn," Willan said. "That's what I decided after you and I and Tiffany met in April. I looked at my life, and I realized that I was the one who was holding myself back most of the time. Sure, there were things I didn't get, and people who seemed to stand in my way, but why did I let these things stop me? Why did I quit? Why didn't I keep working until things started to fall the way I wanted them to? Why didn't I change my attitude, which was a big one for me. Because I felt stuck where I was until I could make myself perfect. And I realized that I was never going to be perfect, and I had to go after what I wanted with my flaws and everything."

"You don't have any flaws," Tiffany said, giving her a look like she was examining her to try to figure out what in the world she was talking about.

"I've been fat all my life."

"Not fat. Don't say that," Leiklyn said, cringing.

"I'm just calling it what it is. I've never been a size zero. Or a size eight for that matter. It's always been double digits. And it probably always will be. I just have to learn to live with myself like that."

"I guess diets didn't really work for you," Tiffany said.

"Ha. And there we go. Maybe it wasn't the diet that didn't work. Maybe it was me. And there, see? I'm still seeing those things in me. I'm giving up because I'm not willing to put more work in." She sighed. She really had tried every diet under the sun, and truly nothing had worked. But... "So I think there's two things. First of all, I just need to be happy with myself the way I am. However I look. But also, if I'm determined to do something, then I can't let anything stop me. I just... I just need to want it enough. And I can't quit trying, no matter how hard it is."

"So you keep hinting about these things you really want. Obviously, you've never been happy with the way you look, but other than that?" Leiklyn asked.

"I want a family," she said, softly, because it was her heart, although it came out easily for her friends.

"You need a man?" Tiffany asked, with knowledge in her eyes.

"I guess. At this point, I guess I just want children. A man would be nice, but that isn't even close to happening. I don't need a husband in order to have children, right?"

"So that's what watching Drake's kids has done to you? Made it clear that you want to have kids?"

"They've made me realize I can do it. That was one of the things holding me back. I thought I couldn't. But that's not true. I can be a mom. I can be a good mom. And once Drake and his kids leave, I'm going to start the adoption process. I have the inheritance. I have enough money to pay whatever the fees are. Why not?"

Tiffany nodded. "Why not, indeed. I guess... I guess I love that idea of waking up one morning and deciding that you are going to totally change your life. Maybe I'll do that," she said thoughtfully.

"No better time than today."

"Wait," Leiklyn said, chuckling. "Can't you wait until tomorrow after the wedding? I don't want someone I don't recognize showing up when I'm expecting my best friends there."

"I'll be there, and I'll be super happy for you. Ethan's a great man." Tiffany smiled, although there was still a bit of sadness in her eyes.

Willan nodded. Ethan was a good man. But that was one of the things she didn't have control over. She couldn't make anyone fall in love with her. She could, however, have control and seek out the other part of a family and find some children who would be blessed to have a mom.

Chapter 15

It was a simple wedding.

Drake sat in one of the folding chairs that had been set up in the grand ballroom, Hazel on his lap and Willan beside him. Kimbi sat on the other side of Willan, holding tight to her hands.

Kimbi had always acted like such an adult, but he'd noticed that she got extremely nervous when there were a lot of people around.

Funny he'd never noticed that before, but Willan seemed to relax her, and she'd started acting like a little girl again, which he was grateful for. She'd always acted like she was at least twenty years older than what she was.

He wanted her to enjoy her childhood and being a kid, not feel like she had to be a little princess and Miss Perfect.

He wasn't sure what had caused her to start acting her age again. Whether that was him, or whether that was Willan's influence. Regardless, Willan had been good for his family.

There were no attendants, just Leiklyn and Ethan in front of the preacher. Leiklyn wore a pretty green dress that looked comfortable but not fancy, and Ethan wore jeans and a crisp blue button-down shirt.

Nothing pretentious. Nothing that they had to stress over. There hadn't even been a rehearsal or dinner the night before. Leiklyn had just spent a few hours with her friends talking and having a good time, while Ethan had caught up with his brother and dad.

Pastor Kane said a few words about love, about the Biblical roles of husband and wife, and about how marriage could make people grow, refining them, helping them to give up their selfishness, because that's what it took in order to put another person first on a consistent basis.

Drake listened closely to the message, realizing that he'd been blaming his divorce on his wife—after all, she was the one who left—but he hadn't been doing anything that the preacher was talking about just now.

Putting someone else first?

Caring about their needs over his?

Being kind to them even when they were unkind to him?

Definitely not. His marriage had been more tit for tat and making sure that Isla didn't get anything more out of it than he did.

No wonder it hadn't lasted.

Pastor Kane went on talking about love, which wasn't anything like the Hollywood definition of love—sleek bodies, perfect hair and skin, lust.

No wonder marriages didn't last. Pastor Kane talked instead about sacrifice, long-suffering, keeping your word regardless of how you felt.

He snorted and felt Willan's head turn toward him.

He cleared his throat a little and glanced over at her, shrugging a bit but unwilling to tell her that he had been snorting because sacrifice, determination, and perseverance weren't exactly high on the list of anyone's idea of what constituted a good romance.

But it's what staying married entailed.

Actually, when he thought about it, the idea that he'd expected to stay married just on the basis of staying "in love" with Isla was ludicrous.

People fell in and out of love all the time. How could he expect to make a lifetime commitment on that?

The ceremony was short and the tables laden with food that people had brought.

"Was there a reason you were laughing during the ceremony?" Willan whispered to him as guests stood up to congratulate the beaming couple.

"There was. But I was hoping I could keep from admitting it to anyone," he said.

She grinned and didn't push further, which he appreciated. Maybe later he'd tell her, but he didn't want to admit right now that his idea of love had been completely out of whack with what would obviously work to keep a marriage together.

Kinda hard to believe he'd been deceived for so long.

They shook hands, and he greeted the residents of Blueberry Beach, the ones that he knew, like Bill and of course Adam who'd worked on the inn a good bit, and his wife Lindy, and their daughter Sierra.

Then there were guests at the inn, who popped in for the wedding, and he loved the familiar and inclusive atmosphere.

"It's crazy. This is such a simple wedding, but there's so much happiness and joy in it," he bent down and said to Willan after they had finished talking to John and Anitra who had walked away with their little girl.

"I know. We make such a big deal about weddings, and yet, no matter how much money you spend, you can't buy the kind of spirit that makes the day amazing."

He nodded. If anyone could buy this, surely he knew people who could. But he'd never been to a wedding where everyone seemed so relaxed and happy and yet everything was so simple—the food homemade, the dress probably out of Leiklyn's closet, not that he was any great judge of women's clothing.

Certainly it was a dress he'd never see Isla in.

His phone buzzed, as though thinking about his ex had conjured her up.

She'd been texting him for the last two days, and he'd been replying only as much as necessary.

Basically, she'd broken up with the nanny and wanted to spend time with the girls. He got the feeling that she felt like she'd made a mistake. She hadn't exactly said that in so many words, but he was reading between the lines.

Their divorce was final, and he had no interest in going back. He hardly thought that sacrifice and commitment and denying oneself and putting your spouse ahead of yourself were things that Isla would have any interest in.

Interesting that in the short time since they'd been divorced, his thinking had gone through such a major shift. He and Isla didn't have much in common at all and never had. However, he wanted to get along with her for the girls' sakes.

So he pulled his phone out and sent back a quick text saying that he'd call her later to arrange for her to have some time to spend with the girls. He hoped that placated her, and she didn't come out to Blueberry Beach like she was threatening to. He shouldn't have told her that he'd bought a lake house.

It was late afternoon when the guests left, the room cleaned and the food taken care of, and Willan and he were able to get the girls home.

"Are we going out to the beach this afternoon?" he asked. It had been their custom since he'd gotten sick, but it was later than they usually left.

"Yes! I want to know what happens in the story!" Kimbi exclaimed, jumping up and down.

He shook his head, amazed at the transformation of his serious and mature daughter.

"I'd love to go, if you don't mind."

"Mind? I love going, too."

"I don't want to keep you from work," she said, like she somehow thought he'd rather go to work than spend time with her and the kids.

"When I first came, I wanted to bury myself in work. I wanted to get away from my life and not think about all the things that had been happening. But since you've come..."

He didn't even want to include his children in it, because obviously he'd rather spend time with his kids than work, but it was her. She was the one who made his life bright again. Made him want to go out on the beach and just hang out.

She was waiting for him to continue, and he didn't know what to say. Technically, she was his employee. And even more than that, she'd never hinted that she wanted anything more between them.

He didn't want to ruin their friendship, and he didn't want to make her uncomfortable to the point where she didn't want to be a nanny for his children anymore.

"I would much rather be on the beach with you and Hazel and Kimbi any day than working, as much as I've been loving just working with my hands and doing something that's helping people."

Was that disappointment that crossed her face? He wasn't sure. He also wasn't sure what that expression meant.

But she nodded. "I've had such a great time on the beach. I haven't had this much fun since I was a kid myself. I forgot how much I love Lake Michigan, and your girls just bring all those good feelings back."

The girls had run off to put their swimming suits on and grab the toys they always took.

"I think days like today are made even more precious because not only did we get to see good friends get married and start a life together, but the summer doesn't last forever. Maybe the wedding reminded me of that too. That life is fleeting. And summer days are even more special, because they're short."

"I think you're right. We know we need to enjoy them, because they're soon gone."

"As soon as you get ready, we'll head out."

Chapter 16

By the end of August, they'd fallen into a predictable routine.

Willan cooked with the girls in the morning and took whatever they made, usually a dessert, in to share with the workers and whoever else was in the kitchen that day at the inn.

Drake's girls loved cooking, they also loved getting to see and sometimes eat lunch with their dad, and Willan often got to see Leiklyn who was back from her short honeymoon.

She tried not to admit to herself that she enjoyed seeing Drake just as much as she enjoyed seeing Leiklyn.

Sometimes Iva May was there as well, and quite often she saw familiar faces from town, either helping, or hanging out talking, or doing what she did and contributing to feeding the bellies of the workers.

The inn was at half capacity, and everyone was excited that work was going so quickly.

Still, summer was winding down, and there was a bit of sadness in the air as Willan sat with Miss Iva May and Leiklyn.

Tiffany was still wrapping things up and was hoping to be joining them sometime in the fall.

As much as Willan loved to see work progressing so quickly on the inn, she also dreaded it in a way.

Drake had enrolled his girls in the public school, somehow managing to use a fictitious name so his real name didn't get leaked to the press.

Willan wasn't sure how all of that worked, but she did know that money helped.

Still, in just a short week, her days would be free again, since both kids would be going to school for the entire day.

The idea made her heart droop in her chest, and she tried not to think about it.

"Are the girls out playing with the kittens?" Leiklyn said as she dished out some of the blueberry cobbler Willan and the girls had brought.

"They are. They're hoping they'll be able to take them home after school starts."

"I think Myla said that they'll be ready to go soon, although it's going to be hard for her. She's so attached." They shared understanding smiles. Myla had taken such great care of Cheddar and her babies. "She has them eating solid food and even using the litter box. She's eager to get them weaned so she can get Cheddar fixed. The vet won't fix her while she's nursing kittens...something about it being too dangerous since she might hit a blood vessel and Cheddar could bleed to death on the operating table." Leiklyn shuddered.

Iva May nodded. "The same thing is true if the cat is pregnant. When we had strays around, it was so hard to catch them between litters. They were either pregnant or nursing kittens, and it was tough to get them fixed when they were too wild to catch easily."

Willan tried to put a positive spin on the thought, but in the back of her head, she was thinking that bringing the kittens home was just going to make it so that there were two more things for her to fall in love with and miss when they were gone.

"How have you guys been liking the lake house?" Leiklyn said, an excited look on her face.

They'd moved before Leiklyn and Ethan had gotten back from their honeymoon, and had been slowly adding furnishings. "It's fabulous. There's still a lot of furnishings to be bought, but I haven't been in a real rush."

"I can't believe he's having you do it all. Are you sure he doesn't...have feelings for you?" Iva May said, sounding a little unsure, like she shouldn't broach the subject.

"I just really think he doesn't care. He was happy not to be bothered with it, and I have to admit it was fun. Price wasn't an object, and I could order anything that I liked. Man, that really does make it fun."

"But you didn't do the whole house?" They'd talked about it a little before, but while she'd seen her friends every day almost, they hadn't had a chance to sit and share a good conversation for a while.

Willan shook her head. "No. It felt like overreach. There are some comfortable chairs for us to sit in the living room, and of course I got beds for everyone and dressers. But there's a den and a room that could be a library or home office and several other rooms like that. I just didn't feel like it was my place to fill all of those areas. Especially if he's just going to get rid of the stuff when he finds someone else." She forced herself to say that last bit, using the word "when" since it was only a matter of time until he left, and she would eventually read some gossip column and learn he had a new flame.

"I've seen you guys out by the lake in the afternoon. It looks like you're having a really great time."

"We have been. We've gone out almost every afternoon. I'm really going to miss it when the girls go to school."

"I think Drake will too. When he comes back to work in the evening, he's always smiling," Leiklyn said, wiggling her eyebrows.

Of course he would be. They always had a good time, whether they were flying kites, or throwing Frisbees, or just tossing a toy for Ruffles to fetch.

They always read some out of a book. Sometimes Drake even acted parts out, and sometimes they did them together.

She wasn't as good as he was, but she was a librarian who'd read to children for years, so she could at least keep his girls entertained, and they didn't seem to notice that he was obviously a professional and she was just a small-town librarian who enjoyed making kids smile.

"How's the adoption process going?"

"I haven't started yet. I thought I would wait until the girls leave. I don't want to be distracted from them. They're my job and my whole focus right now."

"Ladies?" A dark-haired woman, who looked vaguely familiar to Willan, stepped into the room.

Instead of sitting in the dining room, they were actually sitting in one of the sunrooms on the western side of the inn. They had a gorgeous view of the lake, and Leiklyn had decorated the room with comfy couches, a warm rug, and gas logs in the fireplace.

It was one of Willan's favorite rooms. It would be gorgeous in the winter and so cozy.

"You look familiar..." Leiklyn said, her hand tapping on her chin. Then her eyes brightened. "Selena! You and your husband and your two adorable children stayed with us earlier this year. You were one of our first guests."

Selena nodded, then she looked around the room. "You mind if I come in?"

"Not at all," Leiklyn said, with Willan and Iva May nodding in agreement.

Willan remembered she was the lady who had been berating her husband over every decision that he made. She'd felt bad for the husband, and it was one of the instigators she'd used to make herself change. She didn't want to have to have everything perfect or make people's lives miserable so she could have what she wanted.

Not that she judged Selena for her actions. They just made Willan realize it wasn't what she wanted to be.

Selena, who looked tired and careworn, came in and sank down into a comfortable recliner.

"Would you like some blueberry cobbler?" Leiklyn asked, her hand poised above the almost empty container.

"No. Actually, I was kind of hoping to talk to you." The lady's words were hesitant. "I don't know who else to turn to. I don't want to go to anyone I know. I don't want them to know what's happened. I want to try to fix it, and I don't want the world to know."

"What's happened?" Willan asked, alarm bells going through her head. Surely there wasn't an accident where Drake had gotten hurt?

"Ray said he was leaving me!" Selena wailed. "He told me he was leaving or I needed to get my stuff and get out. I didn't know what else to do, so I told him I would come here for a few days and give him some time to cool off. He said he didn't need any time, though, that he just couldn't take it anymore, and I don't even know what he's talking about!" Selena burst into tears, putting her head down and covering her face with her hands.

"Is there another woman?" Iva May asked gently.

"No! Ray would never do that. That's the thing! No one would ever think this of our marriage. It's just... It's making me look terrible, like I'm just this horrible person, because Ray is a rock of stability. I can't believe I'm that bad," she said on a huge sob.

Willan looked at Leiklyn and Iva May, and they all sat there, not knowing what to say.

Finally, Iva May stood up from the loveseat and walked over to Selena, bending down in front of her, putting a hand on her leg while putting another hand around her back.

Selena started crying harder and buried her head on Miss Iva May's shoulder.

Chapter 17

It was probably a good ten minutes before Selena's sobs slowed to an occasional hiccup. By then, Willan was on one side of her and Leiklyn on the other, with their arms around her too.

"Maybe one of you can go and just talk to him? Find out what has made him turn into this man I don't know? Convince him that he's making a terrible mistake and that he's not being fair to me or to our children or to anything! That whatever is wrong with him needs to get fixed."

They were all quiet for a few minutes, then Iva May met Willan's eyes. She kind of lifted her brows.

Willan nodded, knowing that Iva May wanted her to say what happened in her own life.

Her stomach tightened, her throat closed up, and her hands started to sweat.

Selena might not be open to any truth other than the one she felt she saw.

Still, they weren't doing her any favors if they stood here and commiserated with her and acted like all the problems in her relationship were because of her husband.

"Selena?" she said gently.

Selena's eyes, red and swollen, lifted. "What? Will you go?"

"I wanted to tell you something that happened to me this year."

"Your husband left too? Did he come back?"

"I made a discovery about myself," Willan said, still scared, because the look on Selena's face was not welcoming, and in fact her eyes narrowed slightly as she realized the implication of Willan's words, that Willan might be telling her it was her own fault.

"I realized that maybe some of the reason that I didn't have the things that I wanted in my life was because of myself. I don't know the details of your relationship, and I'm not saying that everything that

111

happened is on you. I don't know that, of course. I've only seen you a couple of times here at the inn. I'm just saying that when I sat on the knoll out front, and I looked at the lake, and I thought about the last eighteen years of my life, I realized that a lot of the problems in my life, and the reason I didn't have what I wanted, was because of me. And I also realized that I spent a lot of time blaming other things when I should have been looking at myself all along."

Iva May pulled back just a little, and she rubbed her gnarled hand on Selena's knee. "I saw Willan decide to change. She's not perfect, none of us are. But I saw that she determined that she couldn't change other people, she could only change herself." Iva May paused for a moment, like she wasn't sure whether she was going to disclose this next bit, but then she said, "I think sometimes we justify our actions, even when we know they're wrong, because they're giving us the desired end. And a lot of times," she stumbled a little bit, "a lot of times we think what we've done is worth it because of what we've gotten. But maybe we've hurt other people in the process."

"Are you saying that I hurt my husband somehow?"

"No. They're not," Leiklyn said. "They're just saying so many times we blame other people for our problems when the solution to our problems lies with ourselves."

Selena's eyes seemed to shoot daggers as she looked from one face to the other. Finally, she spread her arms, pushing Willan and Leiklyn aside and practically shoving Iva May out of the way as she stood angrily to her feet.

"You are saying that it's my fault my husband left?" she said, anger dripping from every word. "I came here asking for advice on how to get him to see reason, thinking that I could confide in you ladies and that you would give me good advice. Advice I could use. Something to make him see how terrible he's being and what an awful decision he's making. And you give me some drivel about how this is my fault?"

Selena's eyes filled with tears, but this time they were angry tears, and she stomped to the door. "I'm going to tell everyone I know to never set foot in this place. You guys are awful. You kick people when they're down. You hurt them even worse." She fumbled with the door-knob. "You seemed so nice. I thought you were Christians." She practically yelled that last line, like it was the worst insult in the world, before she yanked the door open, shot through the doorway, and slammed the door behind her.

There was silence in the room as Leiklyn and Willan and Iva May just sat, staring at nothing.

Finally, Willan whispered, "I guess... I guess I didn't handle that very well, did I?"

"You handled it just fine. We said what we could, although probably not what really needed to be said." Iva May shook her head sadly.

"Iva May?" Leiklyn's question came out soft.

"Yes?"

"I've heard you hint before about there being something you did that you really regret. Can I ask... What is it?"

Iva May sighed and pushed slowly to her feet, her knees creaking. She brushed her pants off and turned to look out at the lake.

"It's not that I don't want to tell you, it's that I can't. It involves someone else, and I need to tell that person what I did. Actually, I need to tell two people what I did before I can tell anyone else. And..." She put her hands in her pockets and turned around, looking at her friends. "I know sometimes you think I'm wise, just because I'm old."

"Not just because you're old. You've given me and so many other people great advice!" Leiklyn cried.

Willan agreed. "I always listen to you talk and wish that someday I'll know as much as you do. Wisdom, not knowledge."

"Thank you for your kind words, but I don't feel wise. I never feel wise. And while I know I need to come clean with what I did, I'm scared." She nodded her head, her lips pulling back like she didn't know what else to say. It was fear holding her back. "I know I need to face it. I know I need to be brave. But I'm a coward. Every time I planned on saying something, I've gotten scared and chickened out. I know some-day my opportunities will be over, and I'll have lost all of my chances. But still, I can't get myself to do the hard thing I know I need to."

They were quiet for a bit, and then Miss Iva May blew out a breath. "I guess that makes me exactly the same as Selena. I'm pretty sure she could see that maybe there was some truth in our words, but it's scary to think that you have a lot of problems, and they're all your fault. And fear keeps you from facing the truth, because it's easier and more convenient and less hurtful to yourself if you keep blaming everyone else. It's fear."

"I can add something to that, if I could?" a deep voice said from the entryway.

The three of them looked up to see Pastor Kane standing where Selena had just stormed out.

"Of course, Pastor Kane. I'm sure you have a lot of wisdom to add to that," Iva May replied, with a semblance of her old cheerfulness.

"That's the biggest reason people give for not becoming Christians. They know they need to change. And they don't want to. Maybe it's fear, maybe it's selfishness. Maybe it's the idea they don't want to give up all the fun things that they think they would have to give up in order to be a true Christian. Maybe they think they'll do it later, after they've had their fun. But yeah, change is hard. It's hard for everyone. Fear of change, unwillingness to change, sends people to hell."

Those were strong words, and they sent a shiver down Willan's spine, but she knew he was right. She was thankful that the Lord had given her not just the vision to see that she needed to change but the strength to do it, at least to do the baby steps that she'd taken and hope-fully would continue to take.

"I came in because Myla is outside, and she wanted to know if Leiklyn and Miss Iva May would watch the kids for a bit so she could talk to Willan."

"Of course! I think I have some cookie dough in the refrigerator. Maybe they'd like to bake some cookies with me," Leiklyn said. And she looked at Iva May. "Would you like to eat cookie dough...bake cookies with us?"

"Of course. The children are just darling, and I would love to eat, um, bake with them."

"I wonder what Myla wants to talk to me about?" Willan said as she walked toward the door, then she stopped and turned. "Thanks so much for being willing to watch them. Hopefully this won't take long." If Pastor Kane knew what Myla was going to say, his face gave away nothing.

He nodded at her as she walked out, and she tried not to wring her hands together as she walked to the back porch where Myla almost always was when she was on break from whatever job she was doing.

She reached the porch, and Hazel and Kimbi ran by her, stopping to give her a quick hug before they said, "Myla said we can go inside and see if we can find her mom and Miss Iva May."

"I think they're going to make cookies with you. Why don't you check the kitchen."

The girls squealed as they flew in the house and disappeared.

She walked slowly on the porch and knelt down on the opposite side of the box of kittens where Myla knelt.

The kittens were big enough to climb in and out of the box, but they were currently all inside getting lunch from their mom.

"Hey," she said to Myla. "Pastor Kane said you wanted to talk to me?"

"If you don't mind?"

"Not at all." She put one finger down, petting the kitten that Hazel wanted to call Banana.

"The girls were out here," Myla started slowly, taking a breath and seeming to try to figure out how to phrase her words. "They were going on and on about all the fun things you're doing with them. You guys have been making pies and cakes and cookies and even sandwiches and casseroles for the people who work here. The girls are constantly talking about the things you're doing in the kitchen, and they always ramble on about the furniture you're getting and how you're decorating the lake house, and how you take them to the beach, and how you guys read and swim and play with Ruffles, and just on and on about the things that they do with you."

Willan hadn't realized how much the girls had been talking to Myla as they sat with the kittens and petted them. She supposed more than once, a lot of times actually, she'd been inside talking to Leiklyn especially, and Myla had spent a good bit of time with the girls.

"I'm sorry they've talked your ears off. I didn't realize it. I can make them stay inside if they bother you. When you get a chance to spend some time with the kittens, it's probably annoying to have a bunch of chatter going on around you."

"Actually no. I've loved spending time with them. And I really enjoy listening to them talk. And I heard you say that when they leave, when Mr. Jensen has to go back to making movies, that you're going to look into adopting. Is that right?"

"That's right. I've had so much fun with them this year."

Willan tried to ignore the pain in her heart, the pain she always got when she thought about the girls leaving. She wasn't going to let it bother her. She wasn't going to love them less or hold part of herself back just because she knew it wasn't going to last. That wasn't the right way to live life. She'd end up with regrets, and she knew it.

They both stared at the kittens, smiling as Cheddar stretched out, and their little bodies adjusted to her new position, no one willing to give up their spot on her stomach.

As she settled back down, Myla said slowly, "Would you adopt my baby?"

Willan's heart seemed to stop, and her eyes flew open, her gaze shifting to Myla. "I thought you were going to keep her?"

"I can't do all the things you do. Once I have her, I need to go back to school. I have years before I'm even done with my own childhood. How can I give my daughter or son a good one of their own?" Her words were almost a cry, and she took a moment to compose herself before she started speaking again. "I probably would be depending too much on my mom. She's willing to help me, wants to, but she still has Trent to raise, and she had her kids, you know?"

"Leiklyn has never said a word to me about not wanting to help you. In fact, she kinda gets a sweet smile on her face every time she talks about your baby."

"I know. And that's why I was thinking of you. Not that I want to keep parental rights. I know I need to sign those away, and I guarantee you that I'll sign whatever is necessary so I can't change my mind and try to take her back. But if you had her, Mom would still get to see her, so would I, but she'd be yours."

Willan met Myla's hopeful gaze, a little bit of eagerness, a little bit of fear on her face. Maybe fear of rejection, but she admired Myla for facing it. And asking the hard question.

"I can see that wouldn't be easy for you," she said eventually.

"I want to keep her. Part of me just can't bear the thought of giving her up. But most of me knows that I wouldn't be doing the best thing for my baby if I kept her myself. And even though that's not what I wanted, I know that sometimes I have to make hard decisions and not give myself what I want in order to do the best for somebody else."

The wisdom Myla showed, coming from such a young person, struck Willan, especially after the scene in the sitting room with Selena, who hadn't been willing to do the hard thing, who hadn't been willing to look at herself and see what she needed to do, who hadn't been willing to make herself do what was best for her family.

Quickly, she said a small prayer for Selena, asking that she would see the truth in the words that she'd been given and do what was necessary to save her marriage.

"You're taking a long time to make a decision, and I'm getting worried. If I've offended you, or if you don't want her, just say so."

"No. I want her. I want her with my whole heart and soul, and I am humbled beyond words, humbled beyond anything I can say, that you would think I would make a good mom. I thought I wouldn't be able to. That there was something wrong with me and I would be a terrible mom. I just... I'm just awed by your maturity. By your self-sacrifice. You're so young. And yet... You're making such a wise and unselfish choice. I'm kind of envious, I wish I had been that mature when I was your age."

"I don't feel mature, and I definitely don't feel wise, but I do think I didn't make some wise choices, and I need to make up for them. And the only way I can do that is by thinking about what I'm going to do and then making the hard choice, even if it isn't the choice I want."

"That's beautiful."

Hope had started to blossom in her chest. At Myla's words, it exploded into something that felt like she could barely contain it.

"I'll do it. I'll take her. I'll pay whatever fees we need to pay. I'll take care of it all. And I want to make sure that I tell her about this conversation. That I tell her how unselfish and amazing you are."

Myla smiled a little. It was a sad smile but also a smile of relief. Willan shifted, coming around the box and putting her arms around Myla. "Thank you. Thank you so much. I wanted so much for my baby to have good parents, and I was afraid to put her up for adoption, because I was afraid she might go somewhere where..."

"That you would never see her again?"

"No. I would gladly never see her again, if I knew for sure she was going to a good home, a home that would love her. And not just love her as in saying that they love her, but a home where the mom will take the time to do the things with her that you're doing with Hazel and Kimbi. You're only having them for a few months, and yet you're amazing with them. And they love you. And they're so happy. You are the perfect mom for my baby. And I'm so happy that you've agreed to take her."

Chapter 18

Drake walked into the house at his customary time. He'd come to really enjoy these afternoons, these sweet afternoons, with his girls.

And with Willan.

School started tomorrow, the Wednesday after Labor Day, and he was unreasonably sad.

Wasn't it crazy he was going to miss his family so much?

Still, he had something planned for Willan tomorrow, since he knew that she was going to be sad that the girls were gone, something he was pretty sure would cheer her up. She'd mentioned several times how much she was going to miss them when they went to school, and while he loved hearing that, loved knowing she cared for his daughters so much, it made him sad to think that she would be sad, and he wanted to cheer her up.

"Daddy's home! It's time to go to the beach!" Kimbi ran out, yelling, before she crashed into him, her arms going around his waist. He pulled her close, loving that she ran to meet him when he walked in the door.

He suspected that that was Willan, too. She got excited about his coming home and made the girls excited for it. She never took them to the beach without him, and that made them look forward to him coming home as well.

The beach was a special thing that he did with them.

"You guys all ready? Or you gonna make me wait for half an hour while you comb your hair," he said, ruffling the top of Kimbi's head.

"Daddy! You're messing my hair up!"

"Oh?" He threw an arm out as Hazel came running around the corner.

"Daddy! We have a surprise for you! And you're never going to guess what it is, and we worked all morning on it, and you're going to love it. L-O-V-E, love."

120

"Someone learned how to spell 'love' today?"

"Miss Willan taught me! I said I was scared to go to kindergarten and have everybody be smarter than me, so she said instead of being scared and worrying about it, I could go ahead and just do something about it, so she's been working on my letters all the time, and now she taught me how to spell some words."

"Really?" he said, lifting his head and watching as Willan walked around the corner, a little smile on her face.

"I also told her that reading was near and dear to my heart, and I couldn't wait until Hazel and Kimbi and I can cuddle up somewhere cozy and light candles and read books together."

"But I don't want to do that. I want Miss Willan to read books to me. Because she makes them fun."

"Daddy makes them fun too. Sometimes he acts them out."

"That's nice. But Miss Willan reads all the other words except for Daddy's, and she makes it good too."

"I think they're saying we make a good team," he said with a grin, agreeing.

Willan brought out parts of him that he didn't even realize he had. Better parts. She made him a better person, more in tune with his daughters, more aware of doing things for others, more aware of being unselfish and considerate.

He liked the person he was when he was around her.

He wanted to be with her because she made him better.

In reality, he knew he didn't do the same for her, but some part of him hoped she might like him anyway.

"I think they are." Her eyes shone, and like she had been for weeks now, he was pretty sure that she was happy to see him come home. Almost as happy as his girls.

The things on the inn were progressing rapidly, and while he'd been as flexible as he could with his ex, she'd decided she didn't want to see the girls enough to actually cancel anything on her schedule, so that had been postponed. He'd been happy he hadn't said anything to the girls, so they didn't know that their mother had decided not to see them.

But then his agent had called and asked if his contract could be renegotiated, because the movie he was planning on starting in January might begin filming earlier, if arrangements could be made with everyone.

He had a good mind to say no, but it wasn't right for him to be selfish and hold up production just because he didn't want to leave his idyllic summer home behind.

And have his time with Willan cut short.

And that's one of the things that Willan had done for him.

The old Drake wouldn't have given a second thought as to whether or not he should make the decision that was best for himself. Of course, that's how he had been taught to make decisions. Choose what was best for him.

But as he'd spent more time around Willan, he thought more and more about choosing what was best for everyone and not being selfish, only thinking of himself.

In this instance, he definitely wanted to be selfish, but if they asked him to move the date, he was going to say okay. Work on the inn would be fine, and as much as he didn't want to give up the rest of the time with Willan, it was the right decision.

Shaking that out of his head, he held his hand out. "Are you coming?"

She looked at his hand, and he resisted the urge to snatch it back.

Up until that point, he'd been very good at keeping the line between employer and nanny very firm. Even if they had been more like friends than a boss-employee relationship, there were definitely lines he hadn't crossed.

He was putting a toe across one now.

If she slapped his hand away or ignored it, it was what he deserved.

But her lips trembled a little, and then she looked in his eyes while her hand slid into his and she said, "I'm coming."

His girls were chattering around them, talking about their surprise and what they'd made, but he didn't hear the words, just the sounds, as he stared into Willan's eyes, and the area around them faded away.

He didn't want to leave. He needed to talk to Willan about it.

He couldn't ask her to leave Blueberry Beach. She'd moved back because she'd wanted to be in a small town.

It would have to be him moving to Blueberry Beach. Only he couldn't. He had to go.

"What's the surprise?" he asked, his words seeming to come from far away. He didn't want to talk, just wanted to close the distance between them and put his hands on her shoulders and ask her if there was any way that they could work things out so that they could be together. Maybe he was crazy, but that's what he wanted.

"I want to tell him!" Hazel yelled.

"We agreed that Kimbi could tell, because you told him the secret last time," Willan said, a smile on her face, but she too seemed to be in an almost dreamy state.

He could only hope she was as aware of him as he was of her.

"Daddy?" Kimbi said eagerly.

"Yes, baby?" he said, forcing his eyes away from Willan and looking at his daughter.

"We made water balloons! And Miss Willan said we could take them to the beach and throw them at each other. She said we could even throw them at her!"

"Really? Isn't that going to mess up your hair?" he said, squeezing Willan's hand and teasing his daughter, because she was always yelling at him for messing up her hair.

"Oh, Daddy. Don't be silly. Water balloons are fun. And I can always fix my hair when we're done."

Another thing she'd learned from Willan, since Isla would certainly never teach her anything like that.

"I suppose part of my surprise is I get to carry the water balloons to the beach?" he said, teasing his daughters and winking at Willan, who blushed.

Man, he wanted to stand and stare at her. She was adorable when her cheeks were red and her eyes were guilty.

"You get to carry them because you're the strongest," she said, winking right back at him.

It was almost like flirting.

Were they flirting?

With Willan, his feelings weren't a delicate dance of making sure he didn't say the wrong thing. He wasn't worried about embarrassing himself or having the tabloids find out what a terrible boyfriend or kisser or romantic he was.

No matter how upset she got with him, he was as sure as he was standing there that she would never do anything like that to him.

But flirting?

He'd been careful not to take their relationship there, but...he liked it.

They gathered up the buckets of water balloons outside, and Willan carried the bag that she kept all their books and towels and beach toys in, and the girls walked together ahead of them, Ruffles between them, as they walked out between the dunes to the beach.

"I'm really going to miss this," he said. Nothing they hadn't talked about before, but it was what was on his mind, and he had to say it.

"Me too. I've tried not to let the girls know that I've been sad all day. I know they're excited about school, and I've been trying to encourage that, and make it so that they love school, and only say good things about it, but...I think I'm going to spend all day tomorrow crying. I'm just warning you. I'm going to be a mess."

"Well, about that."

"Yeah?"

But he stopped, because they had just reached the tip of the dune, and a car, bright brilliant red and slung low to the ground, very obviously a sports car, and one that he would estimate to be very expensive, had just pulled up over the small rise and was going toward their lake house.

"Who do you think that would be?" he murmured to himself.

"I'm thinking someone for you," Willan said, irony in her voice. He knew for a fact she didn't know much about cars, but even she could recognize the quality of that one.

"Think so?" One side of his lip tilted up, and he looked down at her, hoping to share a smile with her before he had to face whatever this was.

"I'm sure of it." She nodded her head. "I actually do have millions in the bank, but my money's new money. You're the one with old money, and your friends have it too."

He laughed. They'd joked before about her money being new and his being old. Old being relative since it was only older than hers.

She could laugh about anything, and he appreciated that about her.

"Well, part of me wants to just keep walking over the rise and pretend that we didn't see them, but part of me says that if we do that, they're going to come after us. What do you think?"

She lifted a shoulder. "I'm definitely on the side of the part of you that wants to keep walking and ignore the fact that we have visitors. But I also know that the visitors are probably not for me, and maybe your girls would like to see them?"

He shook his head. "I can't imagine there would be anybody who would drive a car like that and be coming to see us that would know my girls and be visiting them."

"Relatives?"

They'd never talked about his family in Wisconsin. He wasn't super close to them, and there hadn't seemed to be any need to bring them up.

Maybe, if things went the way he wanted them to go and he and Willan could work something out, maybe they would go see his family.

In hindsight, when he had been hiding from the press, he probably should have gone there, but that would be the first place the press would look, and he wasn't entirely sure that he didn't have relatives who would sell him out.

"So...keep walking?" he said, squeezing her hand and making like he was getting ready to take a step forward.

"No. Maybe that's what we want to do, but we both know it's not the right thing."

By that time, the car had stopped at his house, although no doors had opened yet.

"Girls," Willan called, and Hazel and Kimbi both looked over their shoulders. "We have company, and we better walk back to the house and see who it is."

"I've a bad feeling about this," he finally said, unable to put a finger on why there was a sick feeling in his chest, and some kind of invisible force seemed to be pulling his feet toward the lake as they resisted every effort to turn him around. "I guess I don't have to carry this back." He set the bucket of water balloons down. "They were a good idea by the way. I hope we get to them."

Maybe it was his tone, or maybe it was his words, but Willan's eyebrows bunched together, and a concerned look came over her face. "Do you think this might be something bad?"

"I didn't mention that my ex had been texting me, a week or so ago, because I didn't want to talk about it. And I hoped if I ignored her or only answered her as much as I had to, she would go away. But somehow when I look at that car, her face is the image that comes into my head."

Willan's chin jerked up, but she didn't say anything. The smile had completely disappeared from her face, and she tugged on her hand, trying to pull it from his.

"That changes things?" he asked, low, since his children were coming up on them.

"Doesn't it?" Willan asked, her head tilting, a slight bit of hurt in her eyes.

He should have shared that his ex had broken up with the nanny and that they were arranging for her to see the children after the shooting on her film was over. Although that wasn't supposed to be until the end of September.

They hadn't figured out how school was going to factor in, since Isla had been pushing him to hire a private tutor, and he'd been resistant. He wanted his girls to grow up normally, and they had been so excited about school and eager to go. He didn't want to take that away from them.

"I really don't want to," he finally said, but he let her hand go, and she pulled hers back, although she didn't seem to know what to do with it when she had it away from his.

He'd been having so much fun with Willan. He felt like they were friends. He loved being with her, but he should have spent more time nailing down exactly what they were to each other, because if this was his ex, it had the potential to be devastating to their relationship.

And it was all his fault, because he hadn't talked to Willan about anything that was important.

His worst fears were confirmed when the driver door opened. A man stepped out, but it was obvious from the uniform he wore that he was a driver. He stepped back and opened the driver's side passenger door.

One perfect foot in an expensive heel slipped out, and then another one came out beside it. Long, shapely legs, and then his ex-wife stood, exiting the car, looking directly at him.

Isla was there. At Blueberry Beach.

Chapter 19

Looking at the gorgeous, absolutely perfect woman standing in front of the hot red sports car, Willan wanted to turn around and run in the other direction. Hide somewhere. Shove her oversized T-shirt, and her baggy shorts, and her dollar store sandals out of sight.

But that would make her look even more pathetic than she already did, and it defeated everything that she had chosen to do.

She'd made a decision. Today, she got to see whether or not she was going to live by that decision, or if she was going to go back to being what she used to be—always concerned about how she looked, whether she was perfect, and unhappy when she didn't measure up.

It was far more important to be concerned about how she made people feel.

From the front passenger seat, a large good-looking man opened the door and got out. He wore a tight T-shirt, and as he stepped around the front of the car, she noted his skinny jeans and polished shoes.

Beside her, Drake tensed as he took in the man.

Willan wasn't quite sure what that meant. Maybe he still had feelings for his wife and didn't like seeing her with someone else.

Or maybe he recognized the man and didn't care for him.

Whatever it was, she wished she wouldn't have pulled her hand from his. That meant she had to walk beside him without touching him as they strolled back to the car, the girls coming behind them.

Willan had thought they might be excited to see their mom, but neither one of them said anything, and they stopped when they did.

"Isla," Drake greeted his ex. "If you sent me a text telling me that you were coming, I missed it." His tone seemed frosty but not unkind.

"I didn't send you one, because I figured you were up to something like this." Her eyes looked derisively in Willan's direction, then back to her ex-husband. "I suppose this is the nanny you hired?"

"She is," Drake said, his words guarded.

"I saw you holding her hand. You don't have to hide your relationship in front of me. After all, I guess I know a little bit about running off with the nanny." She had a small smile around her lips, although her tone did not hold any more warmth than it had, nor were her eyes anything but shrewd.

They slid up and down Drake's body, which made Willan want to shiver and not in a good way.

Her look was assessing and frank.

"You've lost some muscle tone and put a few pounds on around the waist. Does your agent know about that?" she asked, stepping away from the car and shutting the door.

Drake didn't say anything, and he didn't move as she walked closer to them.

Willan tried to keep her feet from backing away. Her whole body still wanted to run in the other direction, although now less from embarrassment and more from something that felt an awful lot like fear.

Isla's eyes dropped to the children, and she gave a smile that reminded Willan an awful lot of the witch on a children's TV program.

"Hazel and Kimbi. Didn't you miss your mom?" she asked in a voice that sounded almost threatening.

The girls both nodded dutifully, but they didn't move.

Willan wasn't sure whether that was because they didn't want to hug their mom, or whether it was because Isla wasn't the kind of woman that anyone hugged.

"You and I have a lot to talk about," Isla said to Drake. "And I have reservations at a nice restaurant an hour south of here for this evening at 8 o'clock." She sniffed. "There aren't any nice restaurants in this podunk town."

Willan swallowed, wanting to defend her town but knowing that Isla was right. If she wanted a restaurant that took reservations, she needed to go somewhere other than Blueberry Beach.

"And thankfully I brought Hugh, who is the new nanny I've hired for the children. He has a degree in human development and family studies, and he also has child clearances. He's worked at several day cares and three preschools and comes highly recommended."

Willan narrowed her eyes some and tried not to look in disbelief at Hugh, who looked like he was about twenty years old and had movie-star good looks.

"I'd like to see those clearances and the references as well," Drake said, his attention on Hugh.

Hugh's lips turned back in what could only be a smirk. "Of course. I brought them with me because I figured you'd want them. Are electronic copies okay?" he asked as he pulled his phone out of his back pocket.

Drake jerked his head, and his eyes slid to Isla like he was trying to figure out what game she was playing.

She moved closer to Hugh and put her hand on his elbow. "Be a dear, darling, and carry my luggage into the house before you get those up, please." Her eyes slid back to Drake's as she spoke. "You can go ahead and put them in the master bedroom." Her lips turned up in a smug smile. "I assume you two aren't sharing a room for appearance's sake, of course." Her voice was smooth, sultry even, and it sounded like wickedness to Willan.

The man gave her a look and a smile, but it didn't seem to reach his eyes.

It made Willan feel bad for Isla, because whatever their relationship was, it was superficial. He was with her for what he could get from her, and the opposite was also probably true.

Immediately, she tried to shove those judgmental thoughts out of her head.

"I don't recall telling you that you could stay. So just hold up on the bags," Drake said, his tone firm.

The dude stopped. Then, he reached forward, holding his phone out. "Here are pics of my references and clearances. Scroll right." His voice was slow and seductive, and when Willan looked at him, he gave her a wink.

Her eyes widened, and she looked away immediately. There was something about the guy that made her feel like she didn't want Kimbi and Hazel anywhere near him. Not that she had any say.

The thought pulled at her heart and made her neck itch. She wanted to be able to tell these people to leave. But one of them was the girls' actual mother.

Be kind.

Drake had taken the phone, pulled up the references, and squinted down at them.

"You have ID?" Drake asked. Willan didn't sigh with relief, but she wanted to. Hopefully he was as suspicious she was.

Hugh reached into his pocket and pulled out his wallet, taking his license out and handing it over to Drake.

Drake looked at it, looked back at the papers, and compared the two of them.

"He looks legit," Drake said, looking at her and allowing her to see the concern in his eyes.

"Do you want me to pack my things?" she asked, not sure what, exactly, he was saying.

"No!" He seemed to come out of the contemplative daze he was in and turned to his ex. "You can see the girls. Of course you can. I've told you that multiple times, but you wanted me to fly out to California, and I told you I can't. I'm busy here."

"Obviously," she said.

He ignored her. "And you didn't want the girls by themselves. You wanted me to come with them."

"So?" Isla said, one slim shoulder lifting.

"So I told you. I had a job, and I couldn't leave. Regardless, if you'd like to spend some time with the girls, you're welcome to. You are not, however, unloading your luggage at my house, and I already have a nanny. She's here, and she's been doing an excellent job with the girls this entire summer. She's their nanny, and that's final."

Willan felt a little bit like she was intruding on a private conversation, and she moved to leave, thinking to walk into the house or go somewhere, anywhere to get away from this open hostility and almost competitiveness that seemed to be emanating off of Isla.

Drake wasn't exactly happy either. She'd never seen him this annoyed.

But his voice hadn't raised at all, and he didn't look angry, just irritated.

His girls pushed closer to Willan as she stood her ground, not wanting to leave if they needed her to stay.

"Oh, I understand. That's the way the wind blows."

"I'm not talking about the wind blowing. I'm concerned about my children and having the very best for them. That's Willan. I think, if we can talk about this, you'll agree. But I don't think it's something that we should discuss right now in front of the children. Now, would you like to spend some time with them? We were just on our way to go to the beach, and we're gonna throw some water balloons at each other. You're welcome to join us if you'd like."

"You're going to throw water balloons?" Isla said, like he'd just said they were going to go eat ice cream on Mars.

"We are. I left the bucket out there, and the girls are looking forward to it. Come on. You'll enjoy it."

He gave her a couple of seconds to make up her mind, then he grabbed Willan's hand, and she was too shocked to do anything other than follow as he turned around and started striding toward the lake.

"Drake!" Isla said in a tone that would stop a freight train.

Drake kept walking. "If you have something to say to me, come to the beach. Otherwise, we'll be back in a few hours."

He threw the words over his shoulder and kept walking.

When they reached the bucket, he grabbed it with his free hand and kept walking toward the beach, waiting until they were on the other side of the rise before he turned to Willan and said, "I'm sorry. I was rude back there, and I hope I didn't embarrass you."

"I'm concerned about the children," she whispered.

Both of them were dragging behind and no longer looked excited or happy about heading out to the beach. Both of them seemed upset.

Whether that was because they saw their parents fighting, or whether they wanted to be with their mom, or because they were hurt that Isla didn't seem to care about them, she wasn't sure, but she just knew the girls were upset.

"Let's get down to the beach and we'll talk to them. I need to cool off anyway. I might take a quick swim first."

"Go ahead."

He dropped her hand and set the bucket down, then jogged toward the water, not stopping when he hit the edge but jogging up to his thighs and diving in.

"Daddy doesn't usually swim without us," Hazel said.

"He's mad, and he wants to go do something so he doesn't keep being mad," Kimbi said, sounding mature and grown up in a way that she hadn't for a while.

"Are you girls okay?" Willan asked, unsure how to broach the subject that she really wanted to talk about, which was their mother. Why didn't they run to her and throw their arms around her, and look happy to see her?

"I'm glad that he didn't let that man watch us. I like you, Miss Willan," Hazel said.

"We have to put up with whoever they decide," Kimbi said, again sounding wise beyond her years.

"For now, that's me." Willan wasn't sure how long that would last, but she didn't see any point in saying that to the girls. She didn't know what the custody agreement was or how that figured out.

She hadn't talked to Drake about the fact that Isla had basically called and told him to come get the girls, that she didn't want them anymore. She wasn't sure exactly what that meant, not for the girls, not for whatever agreement they had in place.

"Does this mean we don't get to go to school tomorrow?" Kimbi asked, sounding like a little girl again, scared she wasn't going to get to do something she'd been looking forward to for a long time.

It made Willan regret that she had hyped up school so much. If she had known that there was a chance that they wouldn't go, she wouldn't have made it sound like such a great thing.

She also wasn't honestly sure how to answer. Would they go to school tomorrow? She had no idea. But Isla didn't look like the kind of woman who was going to come and take her children back.

Drake didn't seem to be overly worried about that either. But that was also something they'd never talked about. They kept their conversations light and uninvolved, and she regretted that now, although if he ended up walking out, it was for the best.

She refused to admit that she wanted his hand-holding to mean that maybe he was thinking that he wouldn't be walking out.

Isla hadn't followed him, and Willan wasn't worried that she would. She wouldn't be able to be on the beach in the shoes she had been wearing, and she didn't seem like the kind of person who would be happy in her bare feet.

So, by the time Drake had taken a swim and was walking out, she and the girls had the blanket spread and their favorite snacks and a book set out. She had started reading to them but stopped as he walked up.

"Sorry I left you. Everything okay?"

She looked up at him, unsure how to respond. She probably had calmed his girls some. But she didn't know for how long.

She was just doing everything she could to let them know she cared. Both of them were shoved up against her side, as tightly as they could be, as she read the story to them.

Drake grabbed a towel, dried off quickly, and plopped down on his side, lying across the blanket at their feet. "I'm sorry about that, girls."

"I don't want that man." Hazel's voice trembled, but her chin stuck out, a trait that Willan noticed was her stubbornness coming out. She wouldn't want to be Hugh if Isla forced him to be the nanny. Hazel could be a handful.

"He probably won't cook with us. And we probably won't learn nearly the educational things that we learn with Miss Willan."

Drake's lips twitched, and Willan had to hide her own grin at Kimbi's argument. The kid was not stupid. In fact, she was quite intelligent, and she was coming at things from an adult's perspective.

"I can see your child becoming a lawyer," Willan said, even though this probably wasn't the time for joking, but it seemed to be the right thing to say because Drake grinned.

"You think?"

"I think so. She has a natural talent there."

"I agree. I can see it for sure."

They smiled, and their easy banter seemed to put the children at ease, even if they didn't quite understand what they were laughing about.

After that, Drake reassured them that he would talk to their mom and do everything in his power to keep them from having a nanny they didn't want. He stopped short of telling them that Willan wasn't going to be their nanny forever, which would probably make Willan cry just as much as the girls.

None of them were ready for that.

They had school starting in the morning, so once they were reassured that they would work things out, the girls were ready to throw water balloons and soon forget, at least for a while, that their parents weren't getting along and their world could be shaken up at any minute.

They didn't rush back but took their time. Not necessarily because they were dreading speaking to Isla, but because it was their last sweet afternoon together.

Who knew what the future was going to bring. It was even more in doubt now that their visitor had shown up.

As they gathered their things up, the girls ran along the edge of the lake, looking for seashells and talking about when they'd be able to bring their kittens home.

"I'm going to remember this summer as one of the best of my life. Thank you for sharing your children with me," Willan said, meaning it with all her heart. There was so much more in her heart that she wanted to say, but she didn't have the words.

"It's without a doubt the best summer of my life as well. And you made it that way. You could have done the nanny thing as a job and set the kids in front of the TV set and had your life. Instead, you put your whole heart and soul into my girls this summer, and you made it amazing for my whole family. Thank you. I...I have so much more I'd like to say to you," he finally said after glancing at the girls and seeing that they were bringing their shirts bulging with shells back up to the blanket. "Maybe talk to me this evening after the girls go to bed?" he asked, low.

"Sure." Willan swallowed at the look in his eye. It wasn't one she'd seen before.

"I have a surprise for tomorrow. Don't make plans," he said quickly as the girls came, chattering about their shell collection and how they wanted to take it to school and show everyone, and asking if there might be show-and-tell at school, and they were hungry and thirsty, and there wasn't time for Willan to say anything more, only to wonder what in the world Drake would be talking about.

Chapter 20

Unfortunately when Drake got back up to the house holding Willan's hand, which she'd allowed, the car was still there, and he could only assume Isla and her entourage were in his house.

Irritation worked up his backbone, but he tried to tamp it down. He didn't want to fight in front of his children. He really didn't.

But he wasn't going to allow her to use her high-handed tactics and manipulate him into doing whatever it was that she wanted him to do.

And he wasn't going to allow her to use their children as pawns. He'd already texted his lawyer, but he was fairly certain that the custody agreement that they'd drawn up after she had announced that he needed to come pick up the girls because they were interfering with her new romance, and that she'd eagerly signed at the time, because it put him on the hook for all responsibility and all expenses related to raising the children, and it also paid her a rather generous monthly sum, even though she was independently wealthy in her own right as the daughter of the owner of a large peanut butter corporation, would hold up against anything she'd say about him.

He hadn't forbidden her from seeing the children in it, but it gave him complete control over them.

It had never been his intention to keep his kids away from their mother, but he did want to protect them from the potential pain of having their mother use them against him.

Still, their nightly routine was interrupted, as they had guests for supper, and Willan also made sure everything was organized for the girls for school, their things laid out. Their house felt crowded with the extra people, even though it was very spacious.

At least Isla hadn't brought her luggage and put it in his room.

While Willan supervised bath time and helped them lay out clothes for school, he walked out on the deck and sat down across from Isla as she relaxed on his lounge chair.

It was chilly, and she was wrapped in a blanket from the couch.

"Who picked this hideous color?" Isla indicated the turquoise blanket around her shoulders.

"Is there a reason you're still here?" he asked, which wasn't how he had meant to start their conversation, but his irritation that she was insulting Willan's taste got the better of him.

"I thought we could spend some time together tomorrow. After all, I told you I was sorry for what I had done, and I've changed my mind. For the sake of our children, we should try to work things out."

He put his forearms on his knees and steepled his fingers together, biting back the words that wanted to come out, which was absolute denial.

He didn't want to fight. But he wanted to be clear.

"If you want to see the girls, you're welcome to. Right now, Willan's helping them get ready for bed. It's their first day of school tomorrow, and they're both really excited about it. I'm sure they would love to hear a few words from you about school, and some encouragement, and maybe a little interest in what they're doing."

Isla gave a delicate snort. "It's school. They're going to hate it, just as I did. But they have to go. I can tell them that if you want me to."

He bit his tongue. "If you don't want to spend time with the girls, there's no need for you to stay any longer. The Indigo Inn is booked solid, so you'd better leave now so you have time to drive a little further and find a hotel down the interstate."

"After everything that we've been through together, Drake. Is this really the way you're going to treat me?" Her eyes filled with tears, and her bottom lip trembled. "Don't you at least want to try to work things out?"

"You cheated on me. You left. You told me to come get the girls because they were an imposition on you."

"Do you really have to hold everything I've ever done over my head? Can't a person make a few mistakes? Don't you know what forgiveness means?"

"I've forgiven you. I don't have any hard feelings about what you've done. In fact, if anything, I'm grateful. I think I've moved in a better direction because of it."

He was being too honest, and she was getting offended. He closed his mouth.

"Regardless, I don't want to fight with you, and I don't want to have bad feelings between us. I'd really like to get along. But I don't want to have a relationship with you again. I think the relationship that we had was lesson enough for me. And I've spent all the time I want to with you. Let's move on from there and just be friends."

His response sounded reasonable to him, and maybe Isla agreed, because although she didn't look happy, she didn't say anything more about trying to rekindle their relationship.

"Fine. Have it your way. I guess the tabloids will have a heyday when they find out that I came crawling back to you, and you wouldn't have anything to do with me. But that's okay." She waved her hand. "We'll need to stay here tonight. Because there aren't any rooms at that inn you talked about, I've already called. And I'm not going to get back in the car and drive for hours trying to find a place that's suitable. I'll use your bed, because there is no bed in the spare room. You're probably sleeping with what's-her-name anyway." Her tone was derisive, with no hint of hurt in her voice.

Drake figured she pretty much didn't care what he did, and he wasn't quite sure why she'd come back wanting to rekindle what they had unless she found out that her marketability in Hollywood was less without him by her side.

He wouldn't know. He hadn't been reading anything and hadn't been keeping up with the latest, but it was possible.

The things that impressed the people in Hollywood were very su-perficial, and it could be something like that.

Regardless, he said, "If I sleep on the couch, will you be gone in the morning?"

He almost gave a long-suffering sigh, because he knew that "morn-ing" to Isla meant two o'clock in the afternoon.

It didn't matter though, because once they took the kids to school, he and Willan wouldn't be around anyway.

The thought made him smile, and he barely registered her nod be-fore he got up, wanting to walk in and see his girls before they fell asleep for the evening.

Tomorrow was a big day for them.

Chapter 21

The kids were asleep. Isla's driver and "nanny" had gone to find a room at a hotel down the road.

Isla was still there, unpacking her things in Drake's room.

If Willan had realized that she was taking over his room, Willan would have given her hers, and gladly. Drake would be far less comfortable on the couch than she was.

Regardless, she didn't realize it until it was too late, so once the girls were in bed, she wiped the kitchen counters, which she'd neglected to do in all the hustle and bustle of feeding extra people and getting things ready for the first day of school. Then, she tried not to nod too eagerly when Drake asked if she would like to take a walk.

She heard him mentioning to Isla from the doorway of his room that they would be out on the beach, and she could text them if she needed anything. Then he opened the door for her, and she walked out ahead of him. He caught up to her when he closed the door and came alongside of her and grabbed her hand, sliding their fingers together.

"Thanks for agreeing to go with me," he said softly.

Why was her heart thumping so hard in her chest? They were just going to talk.

Still, she couldn't keep her stomach from twirling and her mouth from getting dry.

"Did I do something wrong?" she asked, finally, as they reached the top of the dunes and started dropping over the other side.

"No. You've done everything right. That's the problem."

"So there is a problem?" She jumped on that. She knew there was something wrong.

"Well, I guess there is for me."

She still didn't have enough spit to swallow, and the lump in her throat just lodged there, making it feel like she was choking.

Maybe she wanted to stall, or maybe she just hadn't had a chance, but when he didn't say anything, she finally blurted out, "Did you hear from anyone at the inn that I'm going to adopt Myla's baby?"

He stopped short, looking at her, shock on his face. But his words surprised her. "That's brilliant. That's exactly what should be done. I hadn't even thought of that, but you'd be the perfect mom for her baby. She won't have to worry about whether or not her baby is going to be taken care of, because obviously you'd be excellent."

His words warmed her soul. Whatever the problem was, whatever he wanted to say to her, it couldn't counter this amazing, happy feeling the words of praise he spoke gave her.

"I think that's about the nicest thing that anyone has ever said to me, thank you."

Next to Isla, she felt frumpy and ugly, but at least Drake had given her a compliment that really mattered. One that warmed her. One that she cared about.

However he felt toward beautiful women, she would treasure what he had just said for a really long time.

"I guess... I guess it doesn't really change anything for me though," he finally muttered, tugging on her hand and walking down the beach a little.

"What do you mean?" She tried to figure out what exactly he was saying. "You're still leaving?"

"Well, yeah. I have to. I thought they were going to move it up, but thankfully I think it didn't suit the filming schedule for someone else, and so yeah, I'll be filming in January and beginning of February. Hopefully done by Valentine's Day, if not a little sooner."

"Okay." She wasn't sure exactly what he was saying. She'd already known he was leaving at the end of the year.

He took a breath, blowing out, like he was nervous, which was ridiculous. What would he be nervous about?

Finally, he stopped and turned toward her, tugging on her hand to turn her body toward his.

"I guess it's not a surprise to you that I've been falling for you this summer. But for the life of me, I can't figure out how you feel about me." He grunted. "There. Every time I think about saying that to you, I'm sure I'll be dying of nervousness, because I'm not sure I can handle it if you don't feel the same. Please, take it easy on my heart. I've never felt this way before."

Her eyes had to be as big as saucers, and her mouth wouldn't seem to go shut. Not that she really noticed.

"Falling for me?" she finally said, faintly and with so much disbelief in her voice, it sounded like a squeaky question.

"Yeah...what?" he asked on almost a nervous laugh. "Why is that so unbelievable? Am I really that unromantic?"

"Well..." She'd never really thought about him in terms of romance before, and she tried to give his question serious thought.

"In my defense, I didn't want you to think that I was trying to get away with something with the nanny that I shouldn't be. You know, there are laws about employer-employee relationships, plus my wife just left me for the nanny. I didn't really want to step over those boundaries, but...I look forward to our afternoons together. I look forward to any time together. You make life fun. And not in a we spend a lot of money and do a lot of crazy things kind of way. Just being with you is better than being with anyone else. No matter what we're doing. Whether we're cleaning up the dishes after supper or hanging out at the beach together. I even liked it when you brought the girls in a little early for lunch, and you guys all came to where I was working and hung out with me. I looked forward to all of that."

"I had no idea," she whispered. Truly shocked.

They stared at each other for a few more minutes before he finally said, "Please say something. You're making me nervous."

"I...I never dreamed that you might like me too."

"I think I've moved past the liking you stage," he said. "And I'm feeling brave. I think...I think I might be falling for you as well."

"In love? Falling in love?"

"Yeah. I've fallen in love with you."

His words scared her. She wanted to point out all of her flaws. To tell him that she was never going to look like a Hollywood movie star, no matter what kind of clothes she wore. She would never be able to wear high heels and look elegant. She would never have the perfect lips, and her round chin was annoying. Her hair drooped, and...

"What are you thinking? You have the oddest expression on your face."

"I'm thinking, I'm thinking about all my flaws and how you couldn't possibly like me." She didn't want to admit it, wanted to be able to move on, but she didn't want to always wonder what he thought.

"I don't care. Didn't you hear me? What you look like isn't what I've fallen in love with. I fell in love with the person who is fun to be around. Who doesn't get upset when things don't turn out the way she wants them to, whether it's flour on the floor, water balloons in her hair, or an ex-wife who shows up unannounced and tries to take over the house. Whatever it is, you make it fun. You keep a good attitude. You keep us laughing and enjoying life, and not stressing about stupid stuff that doesn't matter. That's what I love about you."

His words were going to make her cry. She blinked, swallowed, and tried not to allow her emotions to ruin the moment.

"Are you crying?" he asked, gently and softly. His hand came out and cupped her cheek, and his face leaned in toward hers. "Are those tears in your eyes?" He squinted, shaking his head. "Tell me they're good tears, please?"

"Good tears," she said, smiling, even as they started to leak out of her eyes, despite the fact that she was trying as hard as she could to keep them in.

"Good tears are okay." He leaned down, kissing her forehead, running his hand over her cheek and back behind her neck. Pulling her toward him. "I've had this conversation in my head so many times. And I always stumble on one thing. I don't want to take you away from Blueberry Beach. But I can't make movies here."

"I know," she said, tempted to tell him she'd go wherever he went, but that wouldn't really be best for the girls, and if she were adopting Myla's baby, she really didn't want to raise her in LA, either. "What about Myla's baby?" she asked, realizing that although he had said it didn't change anything, she wasn't sure exactly what that meant.

"So we'll have three kids. Is that okay?"

"Yeah." She couldn't keep the surprise out of her voice. It was that easy? "Are you sure you want a baby?"

"I think it's a perfect solution for Myla, I think you were born to be a mother. I think...I'll try to be a better dad this time around."

"You're a great dad."

"I've been learning from you. It wasn't always like that. I don't want you to think that I didn't care, but my career was pretty important, and I admit that I thought the children were just as well off with a nanny as they were with me. I feel like maybe I've learned a little bit better, and I don't want to miss these years." He grinned a little. "It's so weird, but I found out I actually like my children. Of course I love them, but their personalities have really come out this summer, and...I think it's because of you."

He grinned down at her, but there was something in his eyes, and his next words confirmed what she was thinking. "I think Isla kind of tamped down their natural exuberance, and Kimbi especially spent a lot of time trying to be somebody she wasn't just to make her mom happy. I really like to see her coming into her own. She's so lovable and sweet."

"She is. And sensitive to what people want. She knows her mom wants her to be serious and mature, and so that's what she is."

"I see that now. Although I didn't until this summer. Regardless, do you think we can make it work?"

He seemed like he was really unsure, but she nodded her head right away. Thinking about her insecurities and how if she ended up with Drake, she would be around Hollywood ladies a lot more than she ever dreamed she would be.

Could she handle it? Would she be confident and comfortable enough about the way she looked and not get jealous or upset, or...there she went again. She wanted to have everything perfect before she said yes.

"Yes. We can work it out. Whatever it takes."

"You know, when I imagined this conversation, that was the best outcome possible, and I barely dared to hope that it would actually happen. I can't believe it."

"So when you imagined this conversation, and we got to that point, and I said the thing you didn't think I would, then what?" she asked, and she was only half teasing.

"Well, then you throw yourself at me, and beg me to kiss you, and plead with me to marry you that second."

"Really? And you enjoyed that daydream?"

He nodded. "I sure did. That was the absolute best outcome, the entire thing."

"What was the second-best?" she asked, her brows crinkled.

He snorted. "You still ask me to kiss you and beg me to marry you, but you didn't throw yourself at me quite as frantically as you did in the best-case scenario."

"Third-best?"

"What are you digging for?"

"I want to choose the outcome where you do the asking, and the begging, and the kissing."

"Maybe we can compromise on this, too?"

"Okay. How about this. I throw myself at you, beg you to kiss me, plead with you to marry me, and you oblige."

He nodded. "Go on."

"And then, when we're done, which... Maybe kissing will last a long time?"

"I'm pretty sure it's going to be a really long time, but I'm open to suggestions for what we should do when we're done."

"We could replay it. After all, you're an actor, and you're able to do this pretty well. We can pretend that we didn't kiss, and you didn't agree to marry me, and at that point, you can throw yourself at me, and beg me to kiss you, and beg me to marry you, or just as good would be for you to get down on one knee, and do the marriage question, and then get back up and kiss me. You can choose."

"Wow. I get to choose. I'll keep that in mind, for several hours from now when we're ready to go with that replay."

"Good."

He looked at her, and finally he said, "I'm waiting."

"You're ready?"

"Do you need me to say take one?"

They laughed, and then she sobered. "I'm not acting."

"Neither am I. I'm just grateful. So very grateful."

"You know, so that we don't have to interrupt all the kissing that's going to be happening here in a couple of minutes, would you go ahead and tell me what you're planning for tomorrow? You said we were going to talk about it, that you had something planned."

"I do. I'm pretty excited about it, too."

"And it is?"

"A surprise."

"Seriously?"

He grinned, looking pleased with himself. Whatever his surprise was, she was going to be pretty happy with it.

"I'm taking you out on a boat. I've rented a yacht, and a captain, just so you don't think I'm piloting that thing by myself, and we're taking a cruise for most of the day. I have us scheduled to be there at nine o'clock, and I figured we better be in by two so we can be at the school to pick the girls up."

"You're taking off work?"

"I sure am. I've been looking forward to this for a long time, and it's not that I didn't want the girls to go, it's just, since it's your first boat ride, I wanted to make sure you would like it first before we took them and had to have our attention on them."

"That's so considerate. Thank you."

"Now, I'm ready if you are."

She grinned, wondering if she actually had the nerve to pull this off. Maybe she should confess that she'd never done anything of the sort before, and then she decided that no, she wasn't going to confess. After all, the man said he loved her, and he said this was the best outcome that he could imagine, and she wasn't going to let her own fears get in the way.

So she gave him a grin and lifted her arms up, stepping closer and putting them around him, squeezing their bodies together, as she said, "Drake, kiss me, please. Actually, forget that. Drake, kiss me now," she said, emphasizing the now, and then she continued, as his head began to lower, "and when you're done with that, marry me."

He laughed as his lips touched her cheekbone, then her nose.

"That was less like pleading and more like demanding." His lips moved down, touching the corner of her mouth. "I think I like it better. Definitely."

She smiled, and his lips caught her laugh as he kissed her, and he was right. It lasted for a really long time.

Chapter 22

Two months later

"I can't believe we get our very own baby," Hazel said as she got in the car in front of the school.

Drake looked in the rearview mirror as she buckled her seat belt and Kimbi popped in the other side.

"She's at home. That's why Miss Willan isn't picking you up today. She brought the baby home from the hospital, and she's taking care of her."

"Did she name her what she said she was going to?" Kimbi asked.

"Yep. It's Serenity."

"Did Banana and Shelley meet her?" Hazel asked, referring to the kittens that they'd brought home shortly after they'd started school.

"They did. I'm not sure what they think exactly, and I think Serenity is going to need to be a little older before she can make up her mind about them as well. But I'm pretty sure her older sisters are going to teach her to love kittens."

"Oh, we will. We'll teach her lots of things. Like how to find seashells, and how to swim, and we'll have to teach her how to tie her shoes too, although Hazel's going to need to learn how to tie her shoes before she can teach anyone to tie their shoes."

"I'm working on it," Hazel said, with a little bit of frustration in her voice. It was the one skill she hadn't seemed to be able to master no matter how hard she tried.

"It will come, honey. Don't worry."

They talked about the baby the whole way home, and the girls practically exploded out of the car when they parked in front of the lake house.

When he'd left, Willan had been in blissful heaven, although she'd also been nervous. Somehow, despite the class that she had taken on everything that she needed to know to mother a newborn, she was still worried that somehow she wouldn't be able to do it.

He tried to talk her into calling her own mother and having her come up and stay with her for a while. Willan had called, but her mom had been uninterested.

Willan's feelings had been hurt, and he felt bad for encouraging her to do that, vowing that he would never do it again. Maybe she understood his girls and their situation with their mother a little more than what he thought she had since her own mom seemed particularly uninterested in her.

However, her friends had already been out, and when he left, they had been sitting with her, cooing and drooling over the baby.

Tiffany was soon moving back to Blueberry Beach, and Willan was already talking to her about babysitting and girls' nights.

"Don't go in too loudly. Eventually, the baby will have to get used to the noise that we make, but we don't want to barge in too quickly today."

"You told us we have to wash our hands first, right?"

"That's right. Just for a while until she gets a little bigger. Right now, she's so tiny that if she gets any germs on her, they could make her really sick."

"It's like the little kittens when they didn't have their eyes open. We weren't allowed to pick them up until they could see because they were too little," Kimbi said, with authority in her voice.

"That's right. We have to be careful with babies, whether they're cat babies or people babies."

The girls walked slowly through the living room, their heads turning and staring at Willan as she sat on the couch.

Her friends had left, probably to give the family privacy as the girls got home from school and met their sister for the first time. They'd seen her in the nursery window at the hospital, but they hadn't held her.

The paperwork had gone off without a hitch, and they were the proud parents of three little girls.

Kind of funny that he made action movies and his family consisted of women.

Not that he minded. He definitely liked it.

The girls washed their hands and ran back into the living room, slowing down as they reached the couch and almost tiptoeing up to Willan who was holding little Serenity.

"She smells good," Hazel said softly.

"Her face is all scrunched up," Kimbi said, eyeing the bundle like she wasn't sure if it was actually a baby or not. "Does she have arms and legs?" she finally asked, tilting her head and looking at the swaddling blankets.

"She's used to being all snuggled up in her mom's belly, and this makes her feel safe and warm when you swaddle her in blankets. We'll take them off in a bit, because we'll need to change her diaper after we feed her."

"Can I feed her?" Kimbi asked eagerly.

"You sure can. Do you want to practice holding her now?" Willan asked.

Kimbi nodded eagerly, and Hazel said, "Me too. Can I practice holding her now, too?"

"You sure can. Kimbi goes first, and we'll give her five minutes, and then Hazel gets five minutes. How will that be?"

The girls nodded eagerly, and Drake helped arrange them on the couch.

The evening was a little stressful, because all the girls wanted to do was hold the baby, which was funny, because Drake was sure they would have gotten tired of her, just sitting there looking at them or lying with her eyes closed, but they didn't, and they had to be pulled away to eat and to get their things ready for morning and to go to bed.

Of course Serenity started crying as soon as the girls were in bed, and he and Willan took turns walking with her until about two o'clock in the morning when she finally settled down.

"I wonder if that's the way every night is going to be?" he asked when they were finally in bed together, Serenity in a cradle at the foot of it, and his wife wrapped up in his arms.

"I don't care. She can cry every night for the next three years, and I will still be the happiest woman in the world."

"That's because I married you two months ago, three days after you first begged me to."

"I didn't beg. I demanded."

"That's right, I forgot. And then you kissed me like there was no to-morrow."

"Is that how that went?" she asked, nuzzling her nose against his chin and kissing his jaw.

"It is. It was a pretty good kiss. You could come act it out again if you wanted to."

"It's two o'clock in the morning, and you want me to relive our first kiss? You're not tired?"

"Never too tired," he said, kissing her temple and running his hand down her back.

"Are you okay with all of this?" she asked, and he could hear the concern in her voice, like she was really curious as to whether he was.

"Why wouldn't I be?" he asked, wondering if there was something that was bothering her.

"I don't know. Just... A lot of my attention is going to be on the ba-by, and the girls already demanded a lot of attention when they're not in school. You might feel slighted. Not to mention, I don't think it's any man's dream to have a screaming baby from eight o'clock in the evening until two o'clock in the morning."

"I guess you could be right about that. I suppose I never really did daydream about screaming babies the way I daydream about you."

"You're silly."

"I'm serious. Daydreams, night dreams, sweet afternoon dreams." His hand trailed lower. "I guess that's what I'm thinking. Sure, a crying baby isn't exactly what anyone wants, but a beautiful family, sweet afternoons together, summer days, cozy winter nights, us, love, laughter...everything. You have to take the good with the bad. Not that babies are bad, necessarily, just I can't expect everything to be perfect all the time, and it would be kind of immature to have second thoughts just because something isn't right."

"You're right. I guess I didn't really think you'd be having second thoughts. I just didn't want you to be irritated or upset or anything."

"I love you. You're beautiful. You make me better. And I can't see that ever changing. Not for me. Not ever."

"Thank you. That's exactly what I needed to hear." And she didn't demand. She didn't ask, and she didn't beg, but she leaned over and kissed him.

~~~

Thank you so much for reading!

To order **Magical Twilights**, the next book in my *Blueberry Beach* series, click HERE[1].

I love to hear from readers! Come join my Facebook Reader Chat[2] and sign up for my newsletter[3]!

---

1.   https://www.amazon.com/gp/product/B09BBXH1DW

2.   https://www.facebook.com/groups/jessiegussman

3.   https://dl.bookfunnel.com/f5u4jxd8r8

Made in the USA
Columbia, SC
06 February 2023

11879421R00089